STRANGE AND SINISTER PATH

A DEAD COLD MYSTERY

BLAKE BANNER

RIGHTHOUSE

ISBN-13: 978-1-63696-006-7

ISBN-10: 1-63696-006-5

Cover design by: Damonza

Printed in the United States of America

www.righthouse.com

www.instagram.com/righthousebooks

www.facebook.com/righthousebooks

twitter.com/righthousebooks

ONE

THE CAPTAIN WANDERED INTO THE DETECTIVES' ROOM looking like a surprised ostrich lost in Times Square at rush hour. He rarely descended from the remote heights of his office upstairs. Now he inched through the room, looking right and left until he saw me watching him. He waved and moved my way. When he was within earshot I said to Dehan, who was reading through cold case files, "Don't say anything rude about the captain."

She frowned at the page in front of her like she wasn't really listening. "Why?"

"Because he's right behind you."

She jumped and looked around. I smiled. "Guilty conscience, Dehan."

The captain still wore his air of ratite uncertainty. "Good morning, you two. How's tricks?"

I offered him no expression and said, "She hasn't come in this morning, sir."

His eyebrows twitched, and he placed a file on the desk. After a moment, he sat and nodded, like he'd got the joke but didn't think it was especially funny. "We have an unusual request from the sheriff of Lee County, in Colorado."

I couldn't think of anything to say, but Dehan dropped the

case she was reading and frowned. "Lee County? Colorado? Really? What's the request?"

"The details are in the file"—he patted the file with his palm—"but in a nutshell, Detectives, Kathleen Olvera, of Rosedale Avenue, just down the road here, aged twenty-three, was found in Lefthand Canyon . . ."

Dehan laughed. The captain looked at her like she'd said something inappropriate. She suppressed the laugh. "Lefthand Canyon? Seriously?"

"There was nothing funny about the way she was found, Detective Dehan. She had been clubbed, strangled, raped, and then decapitated. This was back in 2012. There was some uncertainty over jurisdiction . . ."

I leaned forward. "Why?"

"Because it wasn't clear that she had been killed there."

I scratched my head. "It's not very likely that she was killed here and transported over one and a half thousand miles to Colorado."

"Quite. I agree. And as the actual scene of the crime was never discovered, the local sheriff investigated. However, there was very little evidence, and eventually the case went cold."

"So what's his request?"

"The Denver DA wanted a review of cold cases, and as they were not able to make any progress, and Kathleen was originally from here, he has asked me if I wanted to run it by *our* cold-cases team."

I raised my eyebrows and spread my hands. "Sure. We'll take a look, see what we come up with. But if it turns out to be a Lee County, Colorado, case, we're going to end up batting it right back to the sheriff."

He nodded, then made a peculiar smile with the corners of his eyes. "Have a look. See what you come up with."

He left us and wandered around the detectives' room for a bit, peering at things and smiling with an air of it all coming back to him, then retired upstairs. You got the feeling he'd had quite enough excitement for one morning.

I picked up the file, and Dehan snatched it from my fingers. She leaned back in her chair and put her boots on the corner of the desk. Her legs were as long as an eight-day week. She read aloud while I sat back and enjoyed looking at her.

"Kathleen Olvera, twenty-three, married to Moses Olvera, then twenty-four, of Seven Hills, Colorado . . ."

"Ah!"

"Don't interrupt. Mother of newborn Sin-eed—S-I-N-E-A-D —how do you pronounce that?"

"Shin-aid."

"What is it, Irish?"

"Uh-huh."

"Kathleen, Sinead, these guys are Irish. Okay. So according to testimony given by Moses and Kathleen's mother, Melanie Vuolo, in July of 2012, Kathleen was suffering from postpartum depression and decided to take a few days and go visit Moses' parents, in Seven Hills. That was Friday the sixth. The parents-in-law, that's Alfredo and Ingrid, claim she never showed up. A few days later, some trekkers found her body abandoned in the woods and called the sheriff. He administered a rape kit because her clothes were in disarray. Her blouse had been ripped and the zipper on her skirt was broken . . ."

"What?"

She glanced at me. "The zipper on her skirt had been broken." She continued reading. "Only one of her shoes was found at the scene. The other was recovered later, on the Lee Hill Road, half a mile outside Boulder."

"Hmmm . . ."

"Shut up. The rape kit established that she had had sex before being killed. Impossible to tell whether it was consensual or not because, after a week in the open, in warm weather, the body was badly deteriorated and partly eaten by animals. The semen was too deteriorated and contaminated to provide a hit. The head was found about six feet from the body . . ." She pulled out an eight-by-ten photograph, examined it, and tossed it over to me. "It had been severed surgically, with a single, clean cut, no hacking or sawing. The weapon was not found. There was evidence of blunt force trauma to the back of the head, premortem." She sighed. "A few initial suspects . . ."

I held up a hand. "Stop there. Let's not follow the same mistaken tracks that they did. Let's pursue our own thoughts. Anything strike you? Where do you want to start?"

We stared at each other for a few long seconds. It was a habit we had got into which irritated other people, but it helped us to think. Eventually she said, "Let's talk to the mother. She lives on Commonwealth Avenue"—she checked the file—"and so do Isaac and Anne-Marie. That's Moses' brother and his wife. They seem to have been a close-knit family." She shrugged. "Catholics. Kathleen's postpartum depression seems to be what sent her off to Colorado, and eventually her death. One person she is most likely to have talked to about it is her mother. Let's start there."

"Hmmm . . ."

"You've never been a mother, you wouldn't know."

"Or a daughter. Let's go, Little Grasshopper. Let's go talk to Melanie Vuolo. It's not a bad place to start."

OCTOBER WAS FEELING TOO lazy after the long, warm months to move over and let in the cold. The leaves on the trees were turning copper but were in denial about their age, and the whole of New York was pretending it was still summer. So we decided to walk the half mile to Commonwealth Avenue at an easy stroll. Along the way, Dehan talked.

"So. She lives in the Bronx but she dies in the Rockies. Is that a random event, or is there a direct causal link? Her husband is from Colorado, she claims she is going to see *his* parents . . ." She shrugged and spread her hands while making a "what can I say?" face. "Maybe they got on well. She has her own mother here, but maybe she gets on with the in-laws. It's not common, but it happens. However that may be, the fact that she never turns up has got to raise the question, was visiting the in-laws just an excuse? Was she really going to meet somebody else?"

"That's two questions."

"Don't interrupt me, Stone. I'm having a flow. We need more facts. We need to know, what was her relationship like with the in-laws? Did she meet her husband in Colorado, or here in New York? If it was out there, who else did she meet?"

"Whom."

"What?"

"Whom else did she meet."

"Uh-huh . . . also, her depression." She shook her head.

"What about it?"

She sucked air through her teeth. "You can't generalize, I know, but the normal thing is, if a girl is depressed after child-birth, she turns to her mother. She doesn't put one and a half thousand miles between herself and her mother. Know what I mean? I mean, if she and the in-laws live *that* far apart, how close can they be, right?"

"Fair point."

"So, my gut, which you are always saying I should listen to, is saying this was not a random killing. She was in Colorado not for the in-laws, but for somebody else." She raised an eyebrow at me. "*Cherchez l'homme.*"

I smiled. "Unless she was a lesbian. In which case, *cherchez la femme.*"

"Right. Here we are. It's that one over there."

It was basically a large, redbrick box with a very small patch of garden out front, sitting behind a very large, old chestnut tree. Directly opposite there was a row of much bigger redbrick boxes, in the form of a complex of apartment blocks that were probably about a hundred years old. They were surrounded by wrought iron fences that hadn't stopped kids from spraying the old walls with ugly, uninspired graffiti. They thought of themselves as artists, but most of them seemed capable only of painting their signatures.

I had stopped to look around while Dehan climbed the steps and rang on the bell. It had once been a solid, working-class area. But decades of Don't Give a Damn had reduced it to a dystopian wilderness where adults hid indoors from a world they no longer understood, while their kids bought into the myth that, in an ugly world, the smartest thing you can do is make it uglier.

The door was opened by a dark, frowning woman in her fifties. Dehan showed her her badge as I climbed the steps.

"Mrs. Vuolo? Melanie Vuolo?"

The woman shook her head. "No, she don't live here no more. She ain't lived here for maybe four years."

Dehan smiled and put her badge away. "Really? Do you know where she's gone?"

"Yeah, she was buying a place up in Morris Park. I got the address somewhere, to forward her mail."

She stared at us a moment, while we smiled politely back. Finally I said, "Could you let us have it?"

"Yeah, is nine twenty, Van Nest. She say is a nice big house, but she never invite me to go see it. She in trouble? I know her daughter died. And the baby was just a few weeks old. That was a big tragedy for her."

I nodded. "Were you friends?"

"No."

"Do you know if her son-in-law moved too? Or are they still here?" I glanced at the block behind us.

"No. They all gone together. Whole family."

Dehan frowned. "The son-in-law moved with the mother?"

"All of them. They all gone together."

We thanked her for her help and started back up the road toward the station, under the big chestnuts and the lazy blue sky. After a while Dehan said, "Catholics and Jews."

There wasn't much I could answer to that, so I smiled benignly at the trees instead. She considered me a moment. When she saw I wasn't going to ask what she meant, she told me anyway. "The whole family thing. With Jews and Catholics, the family acquires an identity all its own, above and beyond the people who constitute it. It's like a corporation. In law, a corporation has its own, separate identity. Catholic and Jewish families are like that. Each family has its own, unique identity. When a tragedy happens, the family takes over. Something great happens, the family takes over. Birth, marriage, death . . . the family."

She paused, stuck her hands in her back pockets, and watched her feet moving beneath her. "Kathleen died. If she hadn't died, she would eventually have become the matriarch, the family figurehead, and people would have said, 'Oh, she's just like her mother!' Instead of that, she died, so her mother took over. And when she moved, I guess she took the whole family with her. Loyalty. Loyalty to the family. It's a big deal for Catholics and Jews. It can be a thing of beauty, or it can be a nightmare."

My car is a thing of beauty. It's a burgundy 1964 Jaguar Mark II, original right-hand drive, 210 bhp. I observed it fondly now as we approached and asked Dehan, "You think that might be relevant?"

She walked around to the passenger side and waited for me to unlock the door, staring up at the cloudless sky.

"It's usually relevant to everything. So yeah, maybe."

I thought maybe she was right. We climbed in and headed toward Morris Park.

TWO

MELANIE VUOLO'S NEW HOUSE WAS A BIG, WHITE, detached clapboard affair a couple of blocks from Van Nest Park. She opened the door and didn't so much look at us as calibrate us. She had mischievous eyes and a naughty smile to go with it. She had red hair, deep blue eyes, and a cute spray of freckles across her nose. She was probably in her midfifties, but looked younger. She raised an eyebrow at Dehan and almost winked at me. Her eyelid fluttered, but she thought better of it and smiled instead. Like I said, it was a naughty smile.

"Yes?"

We showed her our badges.

"I am Detective Stone, this is Detective Dehan. May we come in, please, Mrs. Vuolo?"

The change in her expression said she guessed why we were there. She stood back, watching my face. "Is it about Kath? Have you caught the bastard?"

Her accent was Irish. Not New York Irish, but Irish Irish.

"No, not yet, but the Lee County sheriff has asked us to look into a few things at this end."

She gave a quick nod. "Come in. Would you have a cup of tea?" Before I could answer she looked up into Dehan's face.

"How 'bout you, love? Will you have a nice cup of tea? I'll put the kettle on, so. Go and sit down. I'll be with you in no time. Isn't the weather awful unseasonal?"

The living room was at the back, which made it dark. Through the French doors, the back garden was a luminous green, with the shadow of the house cast long across the grass, touching a large, old wooden shed at the end. The room was fussily furnished, with lots of lace and small porcelain statues of kittens looking nauseating. There were photographs, dozens of them, on every available surface. I scanned them and took note, but Dehan was working through them methodically, one after another. Melanie's voice came to us from the kitchen.

"Would you have some biscuits? What biscuits do you like? Sure, I'll put out a selection, shall I?"

She came in on busy feet with a laden tray and set it on the coffee table in front of the fireplace. "Don't stand there like a couple of trees," she said. "Sit. Milk and sugar? Help yourself to biscuits. The chocolate ones are my favorites."

She laughed for no particular reason as she poured from a large, elaborate teapot. Dehan sat in an armchair, and Melanie handed her an elaborate cup of the same design. Dehan took it and cleared her throat.

"Mrs. Vuolo . . ."

"Mel."

"Mel, what can you tell us about Kath? What made her go to Colorado? How were things at home with her and . . . ? No milk or sugar."

"Mo." She said it as she filled my cup. I sat and she handed it to me. "He's a lovely fellow." Her smile was genuine. "Didn't he just dote on her! *Nothing* was too much for him. God forgive me for saying it, but she didn't know what she had!"

Dehan bit into a biscuit and spoke with her mouth full. "She was depressed?"

"God love her. Ever since little Sinead was born. Between you and me, I think it was an accident. She wouldn't take the pill, you see? And I know you fellers . . ." She waved a finger at me. "You don't like the condoms." She turned back to Dehan. "They say they can't feel anything. Well, I mean, what's to feel? But all the same, that's what most fellers say, according to Mo. I wouldn't know. I always took the pill. Tony, that was my husband, God rest him, he insisted on it. He was awful demanding. An Italian." She turned back to me. "Italians are awful passionate, you know. No offense." She smiled and reached out a hand to touch my knee.

"Mel, tell us about Kath's depression."

"Well, that's what I'm saying! I don't think she was ready to have a baby. Of course, when I was young, we had no time to get depressed, but nowadays it's different, isn't it? And after little Sinead was born, didn't poor Kath get awful low."

Dehan sipped and asked, "How did that affect her relationship with Mo?"

"Well, it wasn't ideal, was it? But then, when is marriage ideal? You know, marriage was not intended to be a magic panacea for happiness, was it?" She turned to me as though I might want to answer. "It was intended to be a partnership, and like all partnerships, there will be good and bad times. But, God love 'em both, things were not easy for them."

"How's that?"

"Poor Mo was working construction. Him and Isaac both. And just after Sinead was born, didn't the fecking foreman go and fire Mo, with a newborn baby at home an' all. He looked everywhere for work, but God bless the boy, hard as he looked, he couldn't find a thing. But even with that, the two of them were inseparable. They just doted on each other. Did everything together, went everywhere together . . ."

Dehan raised an eyebrow. "Except Colorado." Mel looked surprised, but Dehan pressed on. "What's the Colorado connection, Mel? It's an awful long way to go and find a husband."

Mel smiled and sighed. "And isn't *that* the truth! It was Tony, my husband. He was Italian, like I say, and he was crazy about the westerns! Don't they call them spaghetti westerns because the Italians love'm so much? Well! He couldn't get enough of the damn things! So when the girls were small we used to go on holiday to 'cowboy country.' He worked all the hours that God sent and he made a decent living for us. But he insisted, on the holidays, we had to go west: Texas, Arizona, North and South Dakota, Wyoming . . . and in the end we went to Colorado. The girls were twelve and thirteen. And we went to Boulder and every fecking day . . . !" She hooted with laughter. "*Every fecking day* he'd drag us up into the mountains, till we found this town, Seven Hills. Well, you'd love it! Wasn't it straight out of the movies! With a saloon and everything! So we cancelled the B and B in Boulder and spent the rest of the holiday in Seven Hills, in the saloon. Booked a couple of rooms there."

"And that's where she met Mo?"

"And Isaac and Greg."

I raised my eyebrows as I reached for another biscuit. "Greg?"

"Isaac and Mo are brothers. Lovely lads, lovely parents, Ingrid and Alfredo. He was Mexican, but a lovely fellow all the same. And Greg was their friend. His father had a ranch nearby. They was forever together, playing and getting into all sorts of trouble. Happy-go-lucky as you like. Lovely lads. Well, didn't we end up going back every year after that?"

"What happened to your husband, Mel?"

"An accident at work took him from us, 2005. They tried to say that he was careless, but my Tony was never careless. He was meticulous in everything." She sipped her tea. "He left us cared for, all the same, and the company settled out of court. I mean to say, would they settle out of court if it was his fault? I don't think so, do you? Bastards."

"So you continued going to Seven Hills."

"Well, we had to, didn't we? For his memory, and also because the girls loved it there. It's a different world. The freedom! And it's clean, and the people are—no offense—well, they're kind and honest and decent. Not like, you know, a lot of people in the city. And didn't they love their little friends?"

Dehan said, "Kath would have been fifteen?"

Mel nodded. "And I think that was when she fell in love with Mo. It was Isaac at first, when they were kids, and we always said that Isaac and Kath would end up together, and Mo and Pat. And poor Greg, well, he had nobody. But that summer it all changed, and to be honest, I think Isaac was a bit upset. It was okay in the end, because he married Anne-Marie, who's a lovely girl. Just lovely!" She sighed. "But Mo had grown in just a year into a very handsome young man, and he was funny, you know? Had a great sense of humor. All the girls were crazy about him. And she being so upset about her father, he made her laugh." She turned to Dehan. "That counts for a lot, doesn't it, love? When a man can make you laugh."

Dehan's cup was empty. She put it on the table and took another biscuit. "So what happened to Pat?"

Mel's face seemed to contract in on itself. For a moment it looked as though she might start crying, but there was a strength there that held her in check. She waited a moment, then took a deep breath.

"They were both hit real hard by Tony's death. Kath was lucky in that she found love and consolation with Mo. God love him, he was a rock for her. But Pat wasn't so fortunate, and she . . ." She stopped and stared out of the French windows, at the unseasonal sunshine. "She got in with the wrong crowd. Greg was a good lad, but he had some bad friends. Pat started drinking, and then it was the pot, smoking pot, and then it was the hard stuff."

I asked, "Where is she now?"

"She's been dry for a couple of years now, staying off the pot and that. She's out with friends."

"She lives at home with you?"

She burst out laughing. It was a startling sound, almost like the screech of a parrot. "Sure! Don't they all feckin' live at home with me! *Jaysus!* What I wouldn't give for them to all feck off and get their own feckin' places! But they're all still at home with mummy!"

She fell back on the sofa laughing. It was infectious, and I glanced at Dehan. She was laughing too.

When she'd settled a bit, I asked, "Who is 'all'?"

"Ah, love'm. I know life is hard these days, and I don't begrudge them. Mo and, uh"—she hesitated—"and Sinead, they're living at home. He's working at the car dealer and she's started the nursery. Pat's at home, you know, she can't look after herself. She just slips back and starts drinking and smoking again, and mixing with the wrong crowd..."

I smiled, thinking of Dehan's prediction about the matriarch. "What about Isaac and . . ."

"Oh, well, that didn't work out. Him and Anne-Marie broke up."

"When was that?"

"Just a couple of months after Kath . . . you know, was . . ."

I nodded. "I see." I pointed at one of the photographs. Dehan was already nodding, like she had wanted to ask the same question. "I notice a picture there. I gather that's Mo, because there are several of him with Kath. But there he is not with Kath. Who is that girl?"

She looked a bit embarrassed. "Well, that's Anne-Marie." She took a deep breath. "Kath's death was a terrible upheaval for all of us. A second tragedy, and it seemed not so long ago that Tony had died." She shrugged and shook her head. The gesture seemed to say that it was just one of those things. "Mo was devastated. Anne-Marie was just *there* for him. A tower of strength. He'd lost his job, Isaac was working . . . one thing led to another . . ."

I nodded again. "It always does. So Anne-Marie is living here too?"

"Yes. She and Mo were married last year."

Dehan smiled at her. "So you are helping them to rebuild their lives."

"I'm doing what I can, love. In hard times, family has to pull together. All you've got is your family, and thank God we have each other."

I pulled my notepad from my pocket. "We are going to need to talk to Mo. Where can we find him?"

"Him and Anne-Marie are both at the Used Car Mart on 177th Street. She does the paperwork and he sells the cars."

I made a note. "How about Isaac?"

"The last I heard from Isaac, he was living out in Hunts Point. Poor love, things didn't go so well for him. He works for a building supplies company on Halleck Street. Leastwise, he did. He rents an apartment at 841 Longfellow Avenue, bless him."

I glanced at Dehan. She shook her head, so I stood.

"Thank you, Mel. You have been very helpful. We may have to talk to you again at some point, or to Pat. But we'll try not to disturb you."

She told us it was no trouble at all and showed us to the door. We stepped out into the warm fall midday and heard the door close behind us. Dehan walked around to the passenger side of the car and leaned on the roof, watching me unlock the door.

"I need a beer," she said. "And so do you."

THREE

We drove east along Van Nest as far as Bronxdale, then turned north. We had the windows open and cruised at a nice, easy speed, enjoying the temperature. We didn't talk for a bit, till I glanced at her and asked, "Impressions?"

She had her elbow out the window. Her hair was streaming across her face, so she reached back and tied it in a knot at the back of her head. It looked good, but she was totally oblivious to the fact. She was the best-looking woman I had ever met, and also the least vain. She turned to face me and I saw myself duplicated, looking back at myself from her aviators.

"I gotta say, Stone, I didn't get a damn thing." She shrugged. "Mo? Killed her so he could be with Anne-Marie?" She made a face and shook her head. "That's stupid, especially as Anne-Marie went and divorced Isaac just a few months later. Mo could have done the same. Besides, she was killed in Colorado."

I nodded once. "I agree. But we should find out where he was at the time anyway. What about Isaac?"

She made a face like she'd just smelled sour milk. I pulled over and parked outside The Grill House. We pushed in and ordered two beers and a couple of hamburgers, then grabbed a table near the window.

Dehan took a pull and gave herself a froth moustache, which I didn't tell her about. "You know what?" she said. "If Mo had been killed, I'd be looking at Isaac. But that would have happened a long time ago. Why would he kill her after she gave birth? And why would he go all the way to Colorado to do it?"

I took a pull on my beer and sighed noisily through my nose. She pointed at me and grinned. "You have a moustache."

I wiped it away with the back of my hand and smiled back. "That reasoning applies to everybody she knew in New York. I am not convinced that her depression was exclusively postpartum. I think there may have been more going on in her life that we don't know about. There's a connection here between her depression, her trip to Seven Hills, and her death." I paused and pointed at her. "Speaking of which, I was surprised you didn't ask her more about Kath's depression."

"You didn't either."

"You first."

She squinted out the window, like the view didn't quite convince her. "I don't know, Stone. She didn't seem to me to be quite in touch with reality. In fact, I get the feeling she'll go to any lengths to *avoid* an unpleasant reality."

I laughed.

She ignored me and went on. "Kath and Mo doted on each other. They were crazy about each other. He was mad about her and he was so supportive. But when they have a baby, she goes into a depression and goes to Colorado, and when she gets murdered, he marries his brother's wife." She shrugged. "Maybe I'm being judgmental, but that doesn't sound to me like a couple who are doting on each other and are crazy about each other."

I was nodding. "So your point is?"

"I think if I had asked her about Kath's depression, I would have heard what Mel wanted to believe about her depression. And I already know that. The useful information is going to come from Mo and Pat, and maybe Anne-Marie. That what you were thinking?"

"Yup."

The burgers arrived and she took a big bite, spilling salad on her plate. She spoke around a mouthful of meat and bun.

"Sho wha-oo wa' do mow?"

I ate for a while without answering her, watching the anonymous people hurrying past on the sidewalk, wondering how a cute young mother from the Bronx winds up dead, beheaded, and probably raped in the woods in Lefthand Canyon in Colorado. What was the sequence of events that led to her death? At what point did she tip the domino that led, irrevocably, to her murder? Did it happen here, or there?

I wiped my mouth as she drained her beer. "I guess," I said, and leaned forward with a fresh paper napkin, "we go and talk to Mo." As I said it, I carefully wiped the froth from her upper lip. She watched me with a curious mixture of alarm and amusement in her huge, brown eyes. I smiled. "You had a Santa Claus moustache."

IT WAS a short drive down White Plains to East Tremont, and then onto East 177th. It's a grim, soulless part of the Bronx, with gray concrete wastelands as far as the eye can see. And if you move off the avenue, into the back streets, you find decaying red brick and rusting iron, boarded-up windows and graffiti, and the haunted eyes of people who don't even despair, because hopelessness is the only thing they have ever known.

I pulled up on the stark, gray forecourt and we climbed out. The air smelled of exhaust fumes and thrummed with the steady flow of trucks and cars on the avenue and the four freeways that surrounded it. Nobody stopped here. People only passed through, in a hurry.

As we slammed the doors, a man in his late twenties or early thirties stepped out. He was good-looking in a Latin kind of way, with brown eyes, dark curly hair, and a shiny suit that was too baggy and probably too expensive. He smiled with very white teeth and nodded at the Jag.

"Nice wheels. You looking to sell it?"

"Not while I can still drive. I'm looking for Moses Olvera." I showed him my badge. "That you?"

For a moment, he looked worried. "Sure. Is there a problem?"

"We just wanted to ask you some questions about Kathleen."

His eyebrows shot up. "Kath? Well . . ." He looked from me to Dehan and back again. "Kath is dead. She died five years ago . . ."

Dehan frowned at him. "That's why we want to ask you about her, Mo."

He gave a small, nervous laugh. "But that was in Colorado."

I studied his face a moment, trying to read what was going on behind it. Finally, I said, "Is there somewhere we can talk?"

"Well sure, come on into the office. Anne-Marie is there . . ."

"We'd like to talk to her too."

He led us out of the glare and the noise into a cool, shaded interior where everything was shiny: the floors, the plate glass windows, the cars—his suit and his teeth fit right in there. We followed him across the showroom and into a small office at the back. Anne-Marie looked up and smiled as we came in. She was an attractive woman with blond hair and dark blue eyes. She had a natural elegance that was missing in Mo.

"Good afternoon."

I smiled back and showed her my badge. "You Anne-Marie?" The smile faded, and she turned to Mo before answering, like she was checking with him. "Yes. What is this about?"

There was a small table with four chairs around it set to one side, where customers could sit and sign their contracts of sale. Mo gestured us to it and Anne-Marie joined us. As she did so, Dehan spoke.

"The Lee County Sheriff's Department has asked us to make some inquiries on their behalf regarding Kath's murder five years ago."

Mo sat slowly, as though he was somehow deflating. He said, "Oh . . . I thought we had left that all behind us."

Anne-Marie reached out and touched his arm. She held his hand and stroked his hair. "How could it be, sugar? They never caught who did it, did they? They ain't gonna stop till they do." She turned to smile at Dehan. "Are you?"

I said, "The colder a case gets, the more difficult it becomes to solve it. But we never give up."

Dehan put her elbows on the table and sucked her teeth. "What we're really interested in at the moment is Kath's state of mind when she went to Seven Hills. What made her do that, all on her own, with a newborn baby . . . ?"

"Maybe you'd better answer that, sugar." Anne-Marie turned to Mo. "You knew better than I did."

There were some glossy brochures on the table, and now he moved them about a bit, as though he didn't like the way they fit and he was trying to organize them into a better arrangement. "This's kind of come out of left field. I'm not sure . . ."

Dehan had her eyes narrowed at him, like she was trying to peer through a dense fog. "Is that a difficult question, Mo?"

He flushed and looked straight at her. "No! No, I guess not. It's just unexpected, after all this time."

I gave him an understanding smile and said, "Sure. The report said she was depressed."

He nodded. "She was. Postpartum depression. After Sinead was born, she got real low. I didn't know what to do to help her. We were real close always, ever since her pa died. But then everything seemed to kind of change when Baby came along." He shrugged and glanced at Anne-Marie, as though seeking support and confirmation. "We hadn't really planned on having a baby yet. My work wasn't real secure. In fact, I got fired just after Baby was born. And Kath was worried about having kids if we wasn't financially secure. She was sound like that."

Dehan raised an eyebrow. "How did you feel about the baby?"

His face lit up. "Oh, I was over the moon. She was the cutest thing you can imagine. Still is."

I smiled, like I shared his pleasure. "Mo, can you think of anything besides the birth of the baby that might have been depressing Kath?"

His smile faded. "Not really. I mean, we had our money problems, and that was getting to both of us, but we was solid, and we had the family right by us, didn't we?" He turned to Anne-Marie, and she took his hand.

Dehan studied her a moment. "Did she ever confide in you, Anne-Marie? Did she ever talk to you about what was troubling her?"

Anne-Marie nodded vigorously. "Oh, Lord, yeah. We was real close. We was almost like sisters. She would tell me most everything. Even told me a few secrets about this feller!" They laughed, and we smiled patiently. "But when this depression came on her, she just clammed right up. She wouldn't talk to Mo and she wouldn't talk to me. In a sense, that was what started me and Mo getting close, 'cause we used to talk about her, and what was wrong with her. And so we kind of come together."

Dehan raised an eyebrow. "So were you two seeing each other before . . ."

They both erupted simultaneously, and the look of horror on their faces seemed genuine.

"Oh, *Lord* no!"

Then Mo added, "We became close as *friends*. But what really brought us together was when poor Kath died. Then Anne-Marie was a real consolation. She was my tower of strength. But we spoke to Isaac before we ever took it any further than holding hands. We never went behind his back, or Kath's."

I scratched my chin. "Here's the thing we can't understand. What would make Kath take off and travel one and a half thousand miles across the country, when her mother and her whole family was right here?"

He nodded a few times, like he was saying the question made

sense, but had a reasonable answer. "What she said to me and her ma was that she needed to get away from me and Baby for a few days. We didn't have money for her to go on a weekend break or anything, so she was going to go and visit my parents. She got on real well with Ingrid and Alfredo."

Dehan's eyebrows shot up. "Ingrid and Alfredo?"

"My parents."

"I know. You don't call them Mom and Dad?"

He gave a sheepish grin. "I guess we never did. Ingie was kind of strict that way. Ingie, my mom."

"So . . ." I scratched my chin again. "Kath had a good relationship with Ingrid and Alfredo."

"Yeah, they loved her, got on real well."

"When was the last time she had seen them, Mo?"

"Oh, well, that would be a couple of years. Since we moved out here."

"You and Isaac."

"And Anne-Marie."

Anne-Marie spoke before I could ask. "Me and Isaac got married just before we all three moved out together. Mel was real helpful and supportive. She helped Isaac get his construction job before we come. Then *he* helped Mo."

I nodded for a bit, drumming my fingers on the table. Dehan asked, "How did Isaac take Kath's death?"

Anne-Marie's face hardened for a moment, then she shrugged. "It hit us all real hard. He was upset, like the rest of us."

"Do you stay in touch?"

Mo shook his head. "Not really. It was hard for him."

There was something ruthless in Dehan's voice when she said, "Triple blow for him, huh? His childhood sweetheart, his wife, and his brother."

They both looked down at the table. Unconsciously, Anne-Marie reached for Mo's hand. He gave a small shrug. "I guess that's just the way the cookie crumbled. We didn't mean him no harm."

I patted the glossy brochures with my palm a couple of times. "Sure. Listen, you've been very helpful. We may need to talk to you again. I hope that's not a problem."

Mo smiled, but Anne-Marie was still staring down at the table. She hadn't liked Dehan's crack. Mo said, "Anything we can do to help, Detectives."

We left them in the office and stepped out through the shiny showroom and into the mellow afternoon, where the shadows were growing long as the sun began to sink in the southwest. We climbed into the car and eased into the flow of traffic. Dehan eyed me and said, "Isaac?"

I frowned and shook my head, then nodded. "Call him, will you?" I reached in my pocket and handed her the details Mel had given me. "Ask him to come in to the station. I have a feeling he is going to have quite a lot to tell us. This loving, close-knit family is hiding something, and Isaac might be just the man to tell us what."

Dehan was dialing. "Yup. My feelings exactly, Sensei."

FOUR

Isaac showed up at six o'clock. The sun hadn't set yet, but it was hovering over the rim of the world and making the sky blush. I had a uniform take him to an interrogation room, and after five minutes, Dehan and I went up to talk to him.

He was a big guy. If Ingrid was Scandinavian, he had inherited all of her Viking genes. He had big hands, big shoulders, and a big head. His eyes were pale blue, and his hair, which was thinning on top, was a sandy blond. He didn't say anything as we came in, but watched us sit opposite him.

I introduced myself and Dehan. "You want some coffee?"

He shook his head. "What's this all about? This about Kathleen?"

He had a stare like a poke in the eye: simple and direct. I nodded once. "Yup. We're giving the Lee County sheriff a hand, and we wanted to ask you a few questions. That okay?"

"Why not? You talked to Mel and Anne-Marie, and that son of a bitch Mo?" He turned his direct stare on Dehan. "I beg your pardon, ma'am."

She blinked a couple of times and I smiled. "We've heard that Kath was pretty depressed shortly before she died. What can you tell us about that?"

"Plenty."

I leaned back in my chair. "In your own words and your own time, Isaac."

He nodded at Dehan again. "Beggin' your pardon in advance, ma'am, in a nutshell, she was depressed because she realized she'd gone and married one major son of a bitch. Now, I'll try not to swear anymore, but I can't guarantee nothing coz talkin' about Mo makes me real mad. And that's about the size of it."

"In what way was Mo a son of a bitch, Isaac? And what made Kath realize it, just after she had her baby?"

His face flushed, and he looked down at his huge hands on the table in front of him. He made huge fists out of them and did a funny kind of sideways twitch with his head. You could tell he was getting mad. "He's a son of a bitch in just about every way you can name. In fact, there ain't no way in which he *ain't* a son of a bitch!"

Dehan smiled at him. "Try to be more specific, Isaac. Help us out. Give us some examples . . ."

"Oh, I can give you examples, and plenty of 'em. Starting right back when we was kids." He pointed at the wall behind him with his thumb, like that was where they had been kids together. "I am older than him, but he was smarter than me. I don't mind recognizing that. He's smart. But he always used his brains to get the better of me anytime he could. If I had something, that was enough for him to want it more, and take it from me."

Dehan was nodding. "I had a sister like that." She shrugged. "But as we got older we learned to get over it. Now we're friends."

"With all due respect, ma'am, you're lucky. Mo and me never learned to be friends. I tried! Ingie, that's my mom, she beat it into us most every day. Why, she made my ass bleed with a switch more'n once for fighting with Mo. So I tried, but he always had some way of turning things so I was the one who got punished."

I gave a rueful laugh. "It was always going to be you and Kath, right? But he took her away from you . . ."

His eyes went wide. "How'd you know that?"

Dehan was smiling. "We're cops, and it was kind of obvious from what you were saying."

His face went sullen. "When their dad died, and they come up to Seven Hills to get away from things for a bit, Kath had turned fifteen and she'd become real cute. Pretty as anything. But she was broken up with her dad's death. Mo saw his opportunity and got right on in there. It ain't that I didn't care for her. I did. I could see she was real upset, but I didn't have the words the way he did. He just seemed to know exactly what to say and when to say it. I knew he was just playin' her, and she was none too smart, I guess. He just wrapped her 'round his little finger and she fell hook, line and sinker."

He opened his hands and laid them palm down on the table again. "People always said that me and Kath would end up together coz we was the less smart ones. We was good friends, always hung out together in the summer."

He frowned at each of us in turn, as though he was trying to work out whether we understood him or not. After a moment he shrugged, like it didn't really matter. "Pat and Mo was the smart ones. They used to talk and laugh a lot about stuff that me and Kath thought was dumb. They used to pick on us and take the Mickey, called us stupid. But that summer it all changed. I think he'd decided he was moving to New York, and he was going to use Kath to get there."

Dehan asked, "Why not Pat if they got on so well?"

"Coz she was smart, and she knew what he was about. She liked him, but she wouldn't never trust him. Kath was sweet and simple, and after he seduced her, she would'a done anything for him."

It was making sense. "So what happened that summer, Isaac?" He looked at me. "Where did the depression come from if she loved him so much?"

His cheeks and his ears colored. You could see the anger in his face. "I think she began to realize what kind of a man she had married."

"What made her realize that?"

He looked embarrassed and glanced at Dehan. "Personally, I think there ain't many things on God's Earth as beautiful as a woman who is with child. And Kathleen, when she was with child, was the most beautiful thing I had ever seen . . ." He paused to steady his breath. There were tears threatening to spill from his eyes. "But Mo, even though it was his child, didn't see it that way. And once she was pregnant, he lost interest in her."

Dehan was frowning. "Was he ever cruel or violent to her?"

Isaac shook his head. "No, never nothing like that. He was always kind to her, and attentive. He's smart that way. Always charms everybody, even when he don't need to. But he wouldn't sleep with her."

Her frown deepened. "How do you know that?"

He held her eye for a long moment. There was a rage building in him, and I realized in that moment that he could be a very dangerous man when riled. He said simply, "He told Anne-Marie."

I raised an eyebrow. "That's a pretty intimate thing to be sharing with your sister in-law."

He turned his direct gaze on me. "I told you, he always wanted what I had."

Dehan snorted. "He started moving in on Anne-Marie."

"For all his being so smart, he couldn't get a job, till I got work on a construction site. I put in a word for him, and pretty soon we was both workin' and making decent money. We all lived close by. Pat and Mel was on Commonwealth Avenue, just across the road from me and Anne-Marie, and Kath and Mo was at the back, on Rosedale. And for a bit there, it was good. I even thought maybe he was learning to be a decent person. An' that just shows you how darned stupid I can be. Soon as the summer started, and it started getting hot, that work was just too much for him. He kept turning up late, bunking off early, making excuses . . ." He shook his head. "You just can't do that in this kind of job. Two strikes and you're out. I told him, this is unskilled labor, boy! There's a whole line of eager, hungry men waitin' behind you to take your job. You waste the boss' time and you are out!"

He shook his head and pointed a finger like a salami at me. "My mistake? My mistake was thinking that he gave a damn. He got himself fired and lived off of Mel and me, and while he was pretending to be out lookin' for work, he was visiting with Anne-Marie. Anne-Marie is real pretty, and smarter'n me. I guess she's a lot like Mo, and maybe she just used me as a way to get out of Seven Hills, the way he used Kath. When we was courtin' she was always tellin' me, what she really wanted was to go to San Francisco, or L.A., or New York. When she heard that Mo wanted to go east to be with Kath, she was onto me most every day to go with him." He shrugged. "Once Kath was out of the picture because she was pregnant, I guess she was happy to hook up with Mo. They had more in common than she had with me."

He gave me that direct stare again. "I figure it takes a special kind of sick to stop lovin' your wife because she's pregnant with your baby."

Dehan heaved a deep sigh and sat back in her chair. She crossed her arms and blinked several times like she was ticking off thoughts in her mind.

"If I understand you, Isaac, what you are saying is that, like you, Kathleen realized that Mo was having an affair with Anne-Marie, and that was what put her into a depression."

He nodded at his fists. "I think maybe she figured that once the baby was born, he might go back to liking her. She was a good, servile wife and she would'a done anything for him. But when the baby was born, he didn't go back to her. He just kept right on being his son-of-a-bitch self. She realized it was all over between them, and now she had a baby too. I think she realized it was only a matter of time before he left her."

I nodded. It made a lot of sense—at least, most of it did. I frowned to show that one part of it didn't. "What I don't understand, Isaac, is why she went to Seven Hills. Was her relationship with your parents *that* good?"

He curled his lip, still scowling at his fists. "Not really. I guess they liked her okay, save that she was a papist. They never said much about her one way or another. My folks are old-school Methodist. They don't hold with Rome. They ain't the kind of folks you'd go to to cry on their shoulder. They'd just tell you to accept the Lord's will and pray." He looked up at me to see if I understood what he meant. "For them, if you got a problem, you get on with it and fix it. And if you can't fix it, you pray to the Lord for strength, and try again. We're sent here to suffer, and every problem is a trial of faith. So they don't really see much point in cryin', or talkin' about problems. You just deal with 'em."

"So you're telling me you don't understand why she went there either?"

"She was never really that close to my folks." He studied my face a moment. "She was a sweet, loving person. You know what I mean? She was real tender. She'd do anything for anybody. My folks . . ." He gave a lopsided smile. "My folks is as hard as old boot leather. I don't know why she would go visit them."

Dehan was staring hard at the tabletop, and I knew that she was thinking the same as me. After a moment she said, "Isaac, were you in New York from Friday the sixth of July to Thursday the twelfth, 2012?"

He sighed. "Yeah, I was here all that time. I would never have hurt a hair on Kath's head, but I can't expect you to take my word for that."

I asked, "Is there anybody who can verify that?"

"Yeah, Mo and Anne-Marie, and Mel. We all had a big bust-up after Kath left."

Dehan asked, "What about?"

"Everything was coming to a head. Me and Anne-Marie was having trouble. Anne-Marie had been stayin' with Mel while we tried to sort things out. But during that time, Mo and Anne-Marie had been spending a lot of time together and I was getting mad. We had a big row about it, and when Kath went off to visit my folks, Anne-Marie said she was going to spend a few days with Mo while Kath was gone, to look after him, seein' as he was real depressed. I told her if she went, not to bother comin' back. She said fine, and she went."

We sat in silence for a long moment. There was a piece missing, and I couldn't work out whether Isaac knew what it was or not.

"Can you think of anybody, apart from your parents, that Kath might have been going to visit in Colorado?"

He took a moment to think about it, and when he answered he wouldn't look at us. "I've often wondered. There's only one person, but I don't want to tell you who it is."

Dehan snapped, "Why?"

Now he faced her. "Because I know he didn't hurt her. He's tough and hard, the way folks are up there, but he's a good man, and I don't want to cast suspicion on him."

I sighed. "Isaac, if he isn't guilty, he has nothing to worry about. Sooner or later we'll find out who it is, and it's better for him if we can eliminate him as a person of interest. And, bottom line is, you have to tell us."

I already knew the answer, and I was pretty sure Dehan did too, but we needed to hear him say it, and after a moment he did.

"Greg Carson. He was our friend, part of our gang, back when we was kids. He was pretty sweet on Kath, we all were, but he was only ever a friend to her. He's the only person I can think she would go to see. He was . . ." He thought about the word. "I want to say smarter than the rest of us, but Mo was pretty smart and so was Pat. He was a different kind of smart; kind of mature. Do you know what I mean? You could talk to him and he would listen. Then, whatever he said to you, you could rely on as being right."

"You got an address for Greg Carson?"

He gave his head a little sideways twist. "If I know Greg, he'll be where he's always been, at his pa's ranch, where his pa was before him, and his grandpa and his great-grandpa before him.

Greg don't move. He told us we was crazy for goin' east, and I guess he was right, weren't he?"

Dehan gave a small, sad smile, which dimpled her left cheek. "I guess he was, Isaac."

We all nodded.

FIVE

Isaac left, and Dehan and I stood in the corridor outside the interrogation room staring at each other without speaking. Dehan was chewing her lip. As I drew breath to speak, she said, "One: Mo, Anne-Marie, and Isaac all have alibis for the week in which Kath was killed. Two: it's looking very much like Kathleen went to Seven Hills to meet with Greg." She held up her hand. "It's not certain and we need to confirm it, but it's looking that way. The fact that she apparently lied when she told Mel and Mo that she was going to see her in-laws suggests that she had some ulterior motive—at the very least, she didn't want them to know she was going to see him."

"If she was."

"If she was. Three: unless somebody else pops out of the woodwork, he is as of right now our prime—and only—suspect."

I sucked my teeth for a second. "Prime, perhaps, but not only. There are also Mo's parents. You never know what people are likely to get up to when they start doing God's work."

She pulled a face and nodded. "That's true enough. Either way, this all presents us with a problem."

I nodded and sighed. "Our prime suspects are all over in Lee County, Colorado."

"So what do we do, bat it back and say, 'We think it's this guy, or maybe Alfredo Olvera and/or his wife,' or . . . ?"

I shook my head. "Dehan, we don't really *think* it's Greg Carson. We suspect it *might be* Greg Carson. I think it's premature to send it back to the sheriff, casting suspicion on Greg, when all we have is Isaac's notion that she *may* have been going to see him."

She nodded for a while before saying, "Yeah, that's true. But I don't see how we can pursue the leads we have without going to Seven Hills."

I glanced at my watch. It was just before seven p.m. The captain would still be there. I climbed the stairs with Dehan just behind me and knocked on his door. He smiled amiably as we stepped in.

"Stone, Dehan, it seems like only this morning. Oh wait . . . !" He grinned facetiously. "It was! What can I do for you before I head home in five minutes?"

I closed the door and leaned on the jamb.

"We have interviewed all the available witnesses in the Kathleen Olvera case . . ."

"Good work. And?"

"Some new facts have come to light which the Lee County sheriff could not have obtained, because he never interviewed these witnesses."

"That makes sense, and it was, after all, the object of the exercise. So?"

"The new facts point to one particular person possibly having been the last person to see her alive. She may, in fact, have been going to see this person, rather than her in-laws, as was previously thought. Trouble is, he is in Seven Hills, in Colorado."

The captain opened his mouth, but Dehan was quicker.

"Thing is, sir, we don't think it would reflect well on the department if we kick it back so soon, with only a suggestion that it *might, maybe, possibly* be worth interviewing this person, because he *might* have something to do with it."

The captain shut his mouth again, then said, "Clearly you have talked this over and have something in mind. Let me say that you both know full well I cannot authorize an investigation outside our jurisdiction."

"We know that, sir. But perhaps you could talk to the sheriff, explain we have some leads which we are not sure of but need to follow up, and rather than keep knocking the case back and forth, why not authorize us to talk to some possible witnesses in Lee County. If they prove good, we hand the case back to him, but if they just lead us back to the Bronx, no harm done."

He heaved a big sigh and glanced out the window at the quickening darkness. "It's never easy with you two, is it?"

Dehan shrugged and grinned. "I guess that's why they're cold cases, sir."

He picked up the phone and dialed.

It was cold enough for us to exhale clouds of condensation when we stepped out into the night and headed for my car. As I unlocked it, I looked at her over the roof and said, "You want to stay over? If we push off around five or six, we should get there for breakfast."

"Best offer I've had all year."

We climbed in, and the slam of the doors cocooned us from the cold outside. As we cruised along Bruckner Boulevard, she asked, "Do we need any shopping?"

I ignored the odd phrasing and glanced at her. "I think I have everything. Depends what you want for dinner."

She was staring out the window at the passing lights. "You know what I like?" She turned to face me. "I like moussaka. You like moussaka?"

"I love moussaka, but how long does it take to make?"

"Couple of hours." She looked away again.

"We'd be eating at ten. We have to get up early."

"Maybe when we get back. I fancy making a moussaka. I make a good moussaka."

"Yeah, that would be nice. When we get back."

After a moment I glanced at her again and saw her reflection in the window, smiling. "What's funny?"

"Us. We're like an old, retired couple." She turned to look at me and put on the voice of a Hollywood Jewish mama. "Boiny, watcha wanna eat, Boiny? You want brisket? I could make you some brisket. Or you want we should go out to a restaurawnt?"

I laughed out loud, and we both lapsed into a comfortable silence. Outside, Halloween was in the air, and the vendors were already out roasting chestnuts on the sidewalks. They'd be there till after Christmas. Christmas. The tinsel and the lights were already in the shop windows, and it wasn't even Halloween yet.

I said suddenly, "My wife wasn't like that." She turned to look at me, trying to hide her surprise. "It was more a case of what takeout do we get. And eventually what takeout I would get on the way home."

"Did she work?"

"Yeah. She had a career." I couldn't keep the irony from my voice. "As a part-time receptionist at the dentist's surgery on Morris Park Avenue. She had a five-minute commute on foot every morning."

"You never had kids."

"Uh-uh. She didn't want to limit her career options."

"You bitter?"

I shook my head. "I look back sometimes, and I can't understand how I ever got into that situation in the first place, what induced me to marry her . . ."

We were quiet again. She sat watching the storefronts, with their bizarre mixtures of broomsticks, black, pointed hats, orange pumpkins, and Christmas trees, as they sailed by.

"I've never been married, Stone. But I've seen a lot of people *get* married. Some, a very few, stay together. Most get divorced and then marry again." She paused, thinking. "It seems to me that most people fall in love with, and marry, people who are all wrong for them. And the people who are just right for them, don't turn them on."

"Yup. You got that right."

I pulled up in front of the house, and she climbed out and went up the stairs ahead of me, stamping her feet and clapping her hands, billowing condensation from her mouth like a tall, slim dragon. I let her in, and she headed for the kitchen while I turned on the lamps and pulled the drapes. Her voice came to me from inside the fridge.

"Shall I make a risotto? It's quick and it's nice on a cold night."

I smiled to myself. "Sounds good."

"You got sweet potato? I'll put sweet potato in it. You ever put sweet potato in risotto? It's nice."

"I never did."

"You going to open some wine?"

I went into the kitchen and chose a bottle. I pulled the cork and left it to breathe on the table, then took two beers from the fridge, cracked them, and handed her one. I stood watching her chop onions for a moment.

"The zipper . . ."

She gave me a funny look. "As a come-on, it lacks subtlety."

She scraped the onions off the board and into a pot with olive oil. They hissed and sizzled, and after a moment, the warm, fruity smell reached me. She started cutting a red pepper.

"Kathleen's zipper. It had been ripped and broken. That was what made the sheriff suspect rape."

She nodded. "Yeah, that surprised you this morning."

I shrugged. "I have never raped anyone, but if I was going to, I wouldn't bother with the zip if she was wearing a skirt, would you? I'd just pull up her skirt."

She stared at me a moment, then carried on chopping red peppers. "Huh . . . !"

I went on, "Which means that for some reason, the killer

wanted to make it look like rape. Yet, according to the rape kit, she *had* had sexual intercourse. The sheriff assumed, as he was meant to, that it was nonconsensual. Where does that lead us?"

She stared at me with a face like brain-ache. "That she'd had consensual sex . . ."

I nodded. "But whoever killed her wanted us to believe it was nonconsensual. What would make a killer want the police to think his victim had *not* had consensual sex?"

She threw the peppers in and started chopping tomatoes. "To deflect . . . but . . ." Her voice trailed away.

"In the killer's mind, he has made the association sex-equals-killer, and he assumes the police will do the same. So he wants the police to connect the sexual intercourse with an unknown rapist, when in fact it is a known sexual partner. He also knows that by dumping the body in a remote canyon, the semen will quickly become contaminated, so it will not lead the police back to him. They will look for a rapist."

She stood stirring the mixture and shaking her head.

"There are a couple of big problems with that theory. A, it leads us directly to Mo, and we know that it can't be Mo. B, it assumes a level of forensic knowledge that, frankly, I don't believe Mo is capable of. And what's more, C, we know from Mrs. TMI, Kath's mother, that Mel insisted on using a condom."

I was quiet for a moment, visualizing the scene. "Tearing at a zip is difficult, awkward. Pulling up a skirt is easy. Also, there was evidence of premortem blunt force trauma to the head. If she was knocked unconscious . . ."

She turned from the pot to look at me. "Why struggle with the zipper if she was unconscious . . . ?"

I took a pull on my beer, and she started dicing beef. "Who-ever it was assumed, rightly or wrongly, that the cops would expect her to have had consensual sex with him. So he went to some considerable trouble to make it look as though she had *not* had consensual sex. That strongly suggests that whoever had sex with her, then killed her. We can reduce it to this: the killer did not want the cops to know that she had had consensual sex with him." I paused until she nodded, then went on. "Now, the next logical step is that he assumes the cops will take for granted that, if she had consensual sex, it would be with him."

She dumped the meat in the pot. It sizzled and she started stirring. Finally, she said, with a touch of impatience, "That follows, but again, it inevitably narrows it down to Mo." She sighed. "Unless . . ."

"Unless what?"

"Unless it was known, among a small group of people, that she was going to have sex with somebody else."

I nodded. That made sense. "If the killer had told his friends she was coming to see him, for example."

She turned the gas down, then rested her ass against the side of the stove and picked up her beer. "Mo is neglecting her. She knows he's screwing Anne-Marie, she's mad at him *and* frustrated. He's not even providing her with a living. Maybe she connects with Greg on social media, Facebook, whatever. One thing leads to another, and pretty soon she is arranging to go see him. She makes an excuse to Mo and Mel, she's depressed and she's going for a few days to see Ingrid and Alfredo. She goes to see Greg. They hit the sack and then something goes wrong. He kills her and tries to make it look like rape."

I turned it over in my head. "That is pretty persuasive. There is no apparent motive, but it's still persuasive."

She held out her bottle and we chinked.

She poured a cup of rice into the pot and started stirring it in, coating the grains with the oil and herbs and the juice from the meat. "Relationships," she said, absently. "Pays to be single, huh?"

I watched her stir for a bit. She added the water and there was a big hiss. I sighed and spoke half to myself.

"I guess. Or at least make smart choices."

SIX

WE SET OUT BEFORE DAWN AND TOOK THE I-80, VIA Chicago and Nebraska. It was a grueling twenty-six-hour drive to Boulder, but because New York is two hours ahead of Colorado, according to my watch, we arrived twenty-four hours after we set out, at six a.m. We took it in turns, doing six-hour shifts, driving all through the day, watching the landscape turn flat and endless, and then through the night, watching the sky turn from blue to black. I reckon each of us got about five or six hours of uncomfortable, broken sleep. Dehan took the last leg, from Kearney to Boulder, and woke me just before sunup at a service station outside town. We had a drowsy breakfast of pancakes and weak coffee while we watched the sky turn pale dark blue, and then pink, through the plate glass windows, to the slow, rhythmic swish of passing headlamps in the dawn.

After that it was an hour's crawl up into the mountains along Sunshine Canyon Drive, among dense pine woods that sprawled for miles over steep slopes of yellow earth, partially covered in a thick carpet of brown needles. I drove while she napped, and at ten minutes after eight, we rounded a bend and entered Seven Hills. It was a small, shaded town nestled among wooded slopes that didn't seem to have changed much since the Civil War. I could see why Alfredo had fallen in love with it. There was a broad main street with what looked like a general store, a post office, and a saloon, with various other small businesses flanking them. Most of the buildings were either clapboard or log, with only the odd brick construction here and there. It only lacked the horses to make it perfect, but they'd been replaced by pickup trucks.

The Wagon Wheel Motel stood on the right, just before town. I pulled into the lot out front and saw the sheriff's Dodge was already there. I'd called him the night before to let him know we'd be here for breakfast. I killed the engine and sat for a moment looking at Dehan. She spoke without opening her eyes.

"Are we there yet?"

"Yup, and so is the sheriff, by the looks of it."

"Okay." She opened her eyes and stretched. We climbed out into a bright, frosty morning, breathing clouds of condensation into the cold air. Dehan stamped and slapped her arms while I grabbed our bags from the trunk, and we made our way up the wooden steps and into the warm lobby. It wasn't what I had expected.

A big, iron, wood-burning stove stood on the left opposite a heavy reception desk made of hewn, highly polished logs. Beyond the stove, the room opened out into a comfortable lounge with a bar, a dining room, and plate glass windows with panoramic views of the mountains. It was more like a hotel than a motel. Dehan went and warmed her ass by the fire while I checked us in. The landlord, who went by the name of Ned, was a portly man in his fifties with a blond moustache and complacent, pale blue eyes.

As I signed the register, I told him, "It's a nice place. Business must be good."

"We get skiers in the winter," he said, "and Wild-West enthusiasts in the summer. We do okay because we make the effort, but on the whole it's pretty quiet around these parts."

"How about Lefthand Canyon? That easy to get to from here?"

He frowned like he didn't like the question and didn't understand why I would ask it. "Well, that ain't far as the crow flies, but unless you're a crow"—he laughed like that was funny and I pretended I thought it was—"you got to go pretty far out of your way, up to Gold Hill, and then take a dirt track. Otherwise you have to go down to Boulder and take Lefthand Canyon Drive. Some trekkers go there . . ."

He shrugged and gave me a look that said he didn't like talking about Lefthand Canyon.

"Not a place you'd recommend, huh?"

"It's a place you'd only really go if you had a particular reason. And most folks don't have a particular reason for going there, if you see what I mean." He pointed through to the bar. "Sheriff Watson's wait'n' on you in the lounge. I took the liberty of putting you upstairs instead of one of the cabins. You'll find it's more comfortable in the cold weather. I'll take your bags up, if you like."

I told him that was mighty civil of him and turned to Dehan. "Watson awaits us, dear fellow. Shall we . . . ?"

She gave me a look you could only describe as baleful. "You know the only thing I hate more than people who joke on freezing, early mornings in the Rockies after a twenty-six-hour drive?"

I smiled. "Nope."

"Neither do I."

The sheriff was sitting at a table by a vast log fire where they seemed to be burning a whole tree. He was an amiable-looking man in his early sixties, with intelligent eyes and the easy manner of a man who makes a point of rarely being in a hurry. He stood as we approached and held out his hand.

"I saw you arrive and took the liberty of ordering you some coffee and some of Elsie's blueberry pancakes. I never come this way without stopping for some of Elsie's pancakes."

We shook hands and thanked him, and sat. The warmth of the fire was welcome. A bright-eyed girl with peaches and cream skin delivered our second breakfast and told us to enjoy it in a way you just couldn't refuse.

As I buttered a pancake, I said, "Sheriff, I want to reassure you that we don't plan to encroach on your jurisdiction. We just want to clarify a couple of points with some people who might be witnesses and then we'll be on our way. If the case turns out to be yours, we'll hand it right back."

He smiled throughout my little speech and then gave his head a little shake.

"I know what your homicide statistics are for the Bronx, Detective Stone, because I took the trouble to look 'em up. But I don't suppose for one moment that you looked up the figures for Lee County."

I was a little surprised at the question. "No, Sheriff, I confess I haven't."

"Well, I can tell you without having to. Last time we had a murder in Lee County was in 1922. And then the fellow who done the shooting was from Denver. I guess we have a small population, everybody knows everybody, and we just don't go around killing each other. Now." He wheezed a laugh. "I know that ain't no defense in a court of law." He put on an absurd voice. "'Your Honor, couldn'a done it coz I'm from Lee County, and we don't do that kind'a thing there!'" He laughed. "But the fact is that my resources, as sheriff, reflect the fact that we ain't had a homicide in nigh on a hundred years."

We watched him stuff a pancake into his mouth, nod with pleasure while he chewed, and wash it down with coffee. There was something almost hypnotic about the slow pace with which he did it.

"Now, what I *do* have is a canyon where people from out of state like to dump their bodies. We've had a lot of bodies dumped in Lefthand Canyon. It's known for it, and it's been on TV. That was before my time. We even had people drive eight hundred miles from Las Vegas to dump their bodies here. Italians, mainly. But when they allocate resources to the county sheriff's department, they don't look at who *dumps* bodies there, they look at where the bodies was killed. So, what I am telling you, Detectives, is the reason I called on you was because we just don't *have* the resources to look into this case."

I drew breath to answer him, but he held up his hand and said, "Now, just hold on one minute. If you're telling me that Seth Brown has gone and shot Pete Svenson on account of Pete makin' improper suggestions to Seth's wife, then I can deal with that. I *have* the resources. But in this case . . ." He shook his head and stuffed another pancake in his mouth, chewed slowly, still shaking his head, swallowed, and drank coffee. Again we watched him throughout, listening to the crackle and spit of the fire. "Well now, that's a whole different matter, ain't it? Because we don't even know that she was killed here at all. And if my experience is anything to go by, she weren't.

"So what am I saying here? I'm saying, if you two want to stay a week, or two weeks, or six months and investigate this murder, and solve it, and take the darn thing off my hands, you won't get no complaint from me. Anything I can do to help, except manpower, all you have to do is ask."

I nodded, watching him, wondering if he was going to start talking again. He didn't, so I said, "Good to know, Sheriff. We appreciate it."

"You want to see the scene now, or you want to settle into your rooms and have a rest?"

I looked at Dehan. She was chewing on a pancake. She swallowed, gave her head a twitch, and said, "Let's do it. I'm a New Yorker, Sheriff. We can eat, sleep, think, work, and become neurotic all at the same time."

We took his truck. Dehan pushed me into the front passenger seat and climbed in the back, where she immediately folded her arms and closed her eyes. We headed northwest along Sunshine Canyon Drive, through the town and out into the wilderness. As we drove, Sheriff Watson talked, with his slow, assertive, hypnotic rhythm.

"If you asked me," he said, "which you didn't, but I'll tell you anyhow, one of the things that really confused me about this case, and you'll see what I mean when we get there, is . . ." He stopped and turned to look at me with a frown, as though I had said something that was somehow incomprehensible. "This Kathleen, I remember her from back when she was a young kid, always used to come here in the summer with her mom and dad. Well, she knew the place. She was familiar with it. Her and her sister and them Olvera boys, and young Greg Carson, they was always goin' on long treks and riding around on bikes, and Greg's horses—adventures, they called them back then. My point is, she knew the place."

He paused and pulled a cheroot from his breast pocket and poked it in his mouth. He took his time lighting it with a green disposable lighter and, when it was burning, carried on talking.

"So, according to her mom, nice lady, genuine Irish, Kath come out here to see her in-laws. No doubt you'll go and see 'em. She's of Swedish stock, old-school Protestant. His great-grandparents were Mexican, Catholics, but he converted so he could marry her. Takes all sorts, I guess."

"You were saying about . . ."

"Anyhow, like I was saying, she was coming here to see her in-laws, for some reason which was best known to herself. Now, Lee County ain't all that big, as the crow flies. But I often think, if you flattened it out, with all the mountains we have, it might be three or four times the size. You know what I mean? You look at it on a map, and you might think, hell, Lefthand Canyon ain't that far away. But boy! When you're done getting there, you've covered maybe twenty miles or more! So, what I'm wondering is, how in the hell did she wind up in Lefthand Canyon, if she was goin' to see the Olveras in Seven Hills?" He stared at me. "It ain't like she got there, to her in-laws, and then left with somebody. She never even showed up. And still managed to wind up in the canyon. That don't make much sense to me. But maybe you and your partner will figure it out."

I nodded. "I had wondered about that. The receptionist at the Wagon Wheel said it's the kind of place you only go if you have a particular reason . . ."

"Ned ain't wrong. And that particular reason, often as not, is something illegal. We found about six bodies there over the years, but we'll never know how many we didn't find."

We drove in silence for a while. The tops of the hills were bathed in sunlight, but the road was in deep shade. After a while I asked him, "What can you tell me about Greg Carson? You said he was part of the gang."

He chewed on his cheroot for a while, then said, "Good man. Known him all my life. Solid, like his daddy and his granddaddy before him. Tough man. Works hard. I never had no complaint about him. Why d'you ask?"

"Where does he live?"

He turned his head to look at me and raised an eyebrow that said he wasn't used to people not answering his questions. I waited.

"He's got a ranch outside Gold Hill. I'll point it out to you as we go by. You got a reason for asking?"

"Yeah. Isaac thought she might be coming to visit him, and not her in-laws. That make more sense?"

Round about the junction with Route 83, the blacktop had been replaced with beaten earth, and for about five minutes we'd been rattling along, leaving a dust trail behind us. Now we crested a hill and began to descend toward a small town that hadn't changed in the last two hundred years. Every house and store I could see was made of logs. The only things that looked out of place were the cars and trucks that dotted the dirt roads. Sheriff Watson slowed as we approached a junction and pointed to his left.

"See that hill over there? That's where Greg has his ranch. Pine Ranch. Take the first left up ahead, and you can't miss it. We're going down here on the right, Lickskillet Road. It's pretty steep. It'll take us down to Lefthand Canyon."

We bumped down the track for five minutes, descending in a steep zigzag. Finally we came to the bottom, to a broad, dusty road bordered by steep, heavily wooded hills.

"I notice you didn't answer my question, Sheriff."

"Does it make more sense her coming to see Greg than Ingrid and Alfredo?" I nodded and he shrugged. "To be honest, Detective, none of it makes any sense to me."

SEVEN

SHERIFF WATSON PULLED OFF THE ROAD ONTO A PATCH of dirt in the shade of some pines, opened the door, and climbed out. I glanced into the back seat and saw Dehan was watching me. She smiled, and we both swung down after the sheriff. He glanced at our shoes and said, "It ain't an easy climb."

He pointed up into the forest. You could just make out an overgrown, beaten track.

"Couple of hikers had been camping in the valley other side of this slope. 'Bout five miles that way is Seven Hills, where we just come from." He shrugged with one shoulder. "Like I said, we drove twelve miles to get here, but it's only five miles away. So they was coming down along this track and they saw what looked like a bundle of rags in a clearing through the trees. C'mon and I'll show you."

The hill was steep, and under the pine needles the ground was soft and damp from what I guessed had been recent rain. It was a difficult climb. It would have been difficult even for somebody who knew the terrain. After about a minute I called ahead, "Is this the only approach? There is no approach from above?"

"Not for a vee-hicle, if that's what you're thinking." He paused for us to catch up. His voice had a strange echo under the dense foliage of the tall trees. "She'd been out here about a week, so it was hard to be sure. But I think there were drag marks. I figure he parked down there where I did and dragged her up, using a tarp. He'd never've got her here from up top." He shrugged, looking up the slope. "Not 'less he came by mule, or horse."

He jerked his head off to the left. "That's the spot where they seen the body, that clearing over yonder."

I drew level with him and peered among the trees. Dehan came up by my side. The ground leveled off for maybe fifteen or twenty feet and, beyond a fallen tree, there was a broad patch, maybe thirty or forty feet across, where there were only deep ferns, but no pines.

"Back in July, the ferns were less dense. The kids was coming down this path and they seen a bundle, beyond that fallen pine there. We don't get a lot of litter 'round here, folks are mostly respectful of nature, so they decided to go and have a look."

Dehan spoke for the first time since the Wagon Wheel. "Can we go and see?"

"Be my guest."

He led us across the brown carpet of needles under the high green canopy. The only sound aside from the crunch of our boots was the sigh of the breeze in the branches up above. There was no birdsong, but there was the occasional brief flutter of wings.

We made our way around the great, fallen pine and he pointed to a large bush. "See that shrub there? That's creeping Oregon grape. Her body was partially under that bush." We trudged across till we were standing around it. "He'd obviously covered her in pine needles, but wild animals, the wind, whatever, they had come off and she was mostly exposed. There was no blood." He pointed at the bush again. "Her neck and shoulders were underneath the foliage, and her head had rolled down into that hollow, at the foot of the slope there. According to the medical examiner, decapitation was postmortem, and most likely on-site."

Dehan said, "No hoofprints?"

He shook his head and smiled. "I did look for 'em, in case you're wondering. But there weren't none. Don't mean he didn't use a horse, or a mule. Like I say, a week had gone by, and being summer, the ground was hard."

We stood in silence for a while. I tried to visualize the scene. It was probably night, and under the canopy of dense branches above, it would have been very dark. I made a mental note to check if there was a moon that night.

"How difficult would it be, Sheriff, for an experienced horseman to ride up and down these slopes in the dark?"

He nodded, still smiling. "Hard. Much easier to bring her up in a truck, wrapped in a tarp, and drag her in. At night, ain't nobody gonna see you." He shrugged. "That's what the Mob do, all the way from Vegas!" He laughed, creasing up his eyes and chewing on his cheroot.

Dehan raised her eyebrows at me. "So, unless the crime is dumping a body, we haven't even got a crime scene."

The sheriff nodded at her. "You see my problem. It's like I said to you back at the Wagon Wheel, this place is used for just that purpose. That's why you won't catch me kickin' up no fuss about jurisdiction. I'm grateful to have you take this darn case off my hands! I can't figure *what* happened!"

IT WAS JUST short of ten o'clock when the sheriff dropped us back at the motel. We watched him drive away, having told us that if we needed him, his office was in Jamestown—seven miles north as the crow flies, fourteen by road.

Dehan led the way inside and stood with her ass in front of the iron stove again, bouncing slightly with her hands behind her back. I said, "I'm dead beat. Let's sleep till lunch, then we can review what we know and decide on a course of action."

She nodded and looked relieved. I hit the bell, and Ned appeared after a moment wearing his look of secret superiority.

"Ready to go up?"

"Yeah, and we don't want to be disturbed till lunchtime."

He winked, which made me frown, and said, "I understand," which made my frown deepen. Then he handed me a key. "It's the last door on the left, with glorious views of the mountains."

There was an awkward moment when Dehan came and stood at the desk and we all stared at each other. Finally, Dehan said, "May I have my key too?"

He gaped and his eyes widened in horror. "Two rooms? I understood . . . I didn't realize . . . I thought . . ."

I scowled at him. "You thought that two NYPD detectives were going to share a room?"

He went pale and swallowed. "I assumed you were the detective and madam was . . . When you said your partner . . . These days, partner can mean so many things . . ."

I sighed. Dehan was staring at me with a complete absence of expression, which was kind of unnerving. I said, "Look, no harm done. Just give Detective Dehan another room and forget about it."

He was rigid. He didn't look complacent anymore. "We are all booked up till tomorrow."

"Is there another hotel?"

"The Saloon is full. Perhaps Gold Hill . . . ?"

Dehan grabbed the key from my hand and moved toward the stairs. "C'mon, Stone. Forget it. If you don't snore, I promise not to bite."

She stomped up the stairs and I scowled at Ned again. "You get me a room by tomorrow or, pal, I'm coming to sleep at your house."

"Tomorrow."

I followed Dehan up the stairs and down a long passage with wooden walls and a deep red carpet. She unlocked the door like she was disemboweling it and pushed in. The room was nice. It was big, with a big, solid bed and a stone fireplace with the logs set and ready to light. There was an en suite bathroom, a chair and a desk, but there was no couch.

I closed the door. "I'm sorry, Dehan. I clearly told him, you can check the reservation . . ."

She gave me that same impossible-to-read expression. "Hey, I'm not contagious. Just keep your shorts on and we'll be fine. I promise to respect you in the morning. Help me take my boots off."

We left our clothes on and climbed under the bedclothes. The last thing I remember before I slipped into unconsciousness was Dehan's sleepy chuckle as she said, "If my Uncle Ben could see me now . . ."

I awoke to the sound of the shower. A glance at the window told me it was about midday. The hiss from the bathroom faded to a trickle and died. Then there were those odd bathroom noises: the rattle and slide of the shower-cubicle door, the clunk of the bathroom cabinet opening and closing, the muffled flop of a bath towel being unfurled and dropping to the floor. I smiled. For some reason I couldn't fathom, the sounds were oddly comforting.

She stood in the door with a white turban on her head, a white towel wrapped around her body, and an idiot grin on her face. She looked shiny and scrubbed.

"How was it for you?" she said. "Did the Earth move?"

"Cut it out."

"I gotta say, Stone, it wasn't like my girlfriends said it would be. I think you need to work on your technique."

I threw a pillow at her and she indulged in what you could only describe as a locker room laugh. She threw it back and said, "Go shower, big boy, so I can get dressed."

Twenty minutes later, we returned to our table by the fire and had a couple of local craft beers and a hamburger each. The peaches and cream waitress asked if we'd like some Colorado oysters while we waited for the hamburgers. Dehan frowned. "Oysters? In Colorado?"

"They ain't really oysters, Miss, they's . . ."

She giggled and I said, "They're bull's balls."

Dehan looked her square in the eye. "Oh, no, I've had more than enough of that for one day." Then she grinned at me. "Huh, Stone?" Peaches and Cream flushed and scuttled away squeaking.

"Dehan . . ."

She pointed at me. "You know what, Stone? Here's what I don't get . . ."

I shifted uneasily in my chair. "What?"

"She's been coming to these parts since she was a kid. She knows people here. She isn't going to just turn up. She has to have told *somebody* she's coming, right?"

"Agreed."

"I get the impression her in-laws didn't even know she was coming." She shook her head and shrugged. "She came by train, but how was she getting from Boulder to Seven Hills? Bus? Car rental? Was somebody picking her up?"

I nodded. "That would make sense."

"Because if she had arranged to be collected from the station, whoever collected her . . ."

"That's our man."

"So we need to see her credit card records, her emails, her Facebook, phone, WhatsApp . . . all her communication for the month of June and early July to see who was meeting her."

I took out my phone and dialed the captain while she kept talking.

"So here's how it looks right now. She's unhappy in her marriage. Mo is neglecting her. She wants to confide in her mom, but we've seen her mom sees the world through rose-tinted glasses and she doesn't want to know about problems. She turns to Anne-Marie, only to discover that Anne-Marie is screwing her husband, and the birth of her baby, instead of bringing Mo back to her side, seems to have driven him further away . . ."

The captain's voice spoke in my ear.

"Stone. How's it going?"

"We might be making progress, Captain. Listen, we need to see Kathleen Olvera's credit card and phone records, WhatsApp, email, Facebook—the whole package—for the months of June and July, 2012. And any other messenger and social media she may have been using. The sheriff here is happy to give us free rein, but the deal is we take the case off his hands."

"Fair enough. I'll see to it."

"Thanks."

I hung up. Dehan kept talking.

"So she's looking for a friend. Isaac . . ." She blew out through her teeth and shook her head. "Isaac is the husband of the woman who is sleeping with her husband. It's like an unspoken rule. If she seeks consolation with him, she has to sleep with him. She doesn't want that. So she ends up connecting with Greg. They talk several times, probably on Facebook, and she tells him what's happened. He tells her to come out and stay with him for a few days. She agrees . . ."

The hamburgers arrived. Peaches and Cream's cheeks were still prettily pink. She told us to enjoy and hurried away.

Dehan sank back in her chair. I said, "Okay, that all sounds very plausible, but we have two problems here. One, why would she tell Mo she was going to see his parents? It would take one conversation between him and them to reveal she had not arranged to go and see them. Two, what is Greg's motive for killing her?"

She bit into her burger and shook her head. She chewed and swallowed while I bit.

"No problem. One, her plan is to go and see them. She will stay the night with Greg and then come and see them the next morning. Two, Greg thinks she has come to have an affair with him, but she is a sweet kid who is still in love with Mo. Either she regrets it and backs out, or never expected to have sex in the first place. She's naïve. She thinks they are just friends. He gets mad and rapes her."

We sat chewing and staring at each other. I swallowed.

"So, while we wait for the captain to arrange the records, we need to talk to the Olveras. Then we go and see Greg."

She nodded slowly. "He's the guy, Stone."

EIGHT

Alfredo and Ingrid Olvera had a severely humorless house on the outskirts of the town. It was a white clapboard affair with a gable roof and a small front garden given over to the cultivation of beans and peas. A simple stone path led through the center of the garden to a plain front door. You could imagine, as you approached that door, that the words "simple" and "plain" figured large in the Olveras' lexicon.

It was Ingrid who opened the door to us. She was probably in her early sixties but looked older. Her skin looked desiccated and leathery. Hair that had been blond was now turning to gray, and blue eyes that must once have laughed now judged the world and found it wanting. She didn't say anything, so I spoke.

"Mrs. Olvera?"

She nodded once. "You must be the detectives from New York."

"This is Detective Dehan. I am Detective Stone. May we talk to you for a moment? We need to ask you a few questions."

"Make it quick. I ain't got long."

She led us through a dead hall to a soulless living room where a round table stood in the center of the floor with four hard chairs about it. Two very basic captain's chairs stood in front of an open fire, which at the moment lay unlit. The room was cold. There was a simple dresser, a writing desk, and a credenza, little else. There were no photographs, no pictures of any sort, and no ornaments. The mats on the floor were basic rush. She gestured us to the table and we sat.

Dehan looked around the room. "Is your husband home, Mrs. Olvera?"

"He's tending to the animals."

"We're going to need to talk to him too."

She didn't react, just sat looking at Dehan with eyes that had grown obstinate through years of denying herself joy. I said, "Would you go and get him, please, Mrs. Olvera?"

She didn't argue. She rose and left the room. Dehan shook her head. "Kathleen wasn't coming here."

"I agree."

"Who would?"

"The penitent?"

We heard the measured tread of shoes on bare boards, and Ingrid returned accompanied by a small, gnarled man with gray hair and a large, unkempt beard and moustache. We rose to greet him and he shook our hands, searching our faces with his pale eyes.

"Ingrid, tea. We have guests." He sat, and she withdrew to the kitchen. "Our home is simple, plain, but we can offer hospitality." There was a trace of an accent, but only a trace. "What is a Christian who does not offer hospitality?"

"Mr. Olvera, we don't want to take up your time. We just have a couple of questions for you and your wife. We are collaborating with the county sheriff's department in the investigation into Kathleen Olvera's murder."

He nodded once. "I know."

"There are a couple of things we are not clear about. Were you aware that Kathleen intended to come and visit you?"

He shook his head. "No. We had no contact with Kathleen, or her sister or her mother for that matter. They were papists. We did not approve of our boys consorting with them, but there was precious little we could do to prevent it."

"And look where it has led them . . ." Ingrid stood in the doorway, watching us with a face like curdled milk. "One of them a drug addict, the other murdered after fornication, and our boys consorting with God knows what whores in Babylon . . ."

"Go back to the kitchen and get the tea, woman." She withdrew. He continued. "Melanie Vuolo is an Irish Catholic, who was married to an Italian Catholic. He was an infantile man, always playing like a child, consumed with idle curiosity about cowboys and the Wild West. Stupid man. And his wife . . ." He curled his lip. "Not a good woman. A painted harlot."

Dehan's eyebrows shot up. "Really? What makes you say that?"

He fixed her with hard, unforgiving eyes. "After her husband died, he was barely in the ground, she was in the bars, drinking alcohol, mixing with the men. Her children in the hotel, alone, and her out in the bars, with men."

Ingrid came back in with a tray. On it there was a plain, undecorated pot and four plain mugs. She set it down on the table and poured. She didn't ask if we wanted milk or sugar. Instead she said, "We told Moses and Isaac not to mix with those girls, for the Lord was surely going to punish them. And he surely has."

Dehan gave her a look that was admirable for its restraint. "With all due respect, ma'am, I don't think it was God that raped, strangled, and beheaded Kathleen Olvera. I think it was a man. And I don't know if God's Law says that her rape and murder was acceptable because her mother drank and used makeup, but the law of the United States says it's a heinous crime. And I have to say, I tend to agree. Now can we clarify, please? Are you saying that Kathleen did not contact you to say she was coming to visit?"

Their faces had gone like stone. He answered.

"She did not. And if she had, we would have told her she was not welcome."

"Because she had stolen your sons from you."

She spoke through pinched lips. "They were young and innocent. Those girls seduced them. They led them away from the path of righteousness."

I said, "And all you wanted to do was lead them back."

"We only try to do God's work. We are simple, plain folk."

"What does God's work include, Mr. Olvera?"

"Whatever God commands."

"And how do you know what God commands?"

He was watching me carefully because he knew where we were going. "It is all written in the Good Book, Detective, and the Sixth Commandment states very clearly, thou shalt not kill."

Dehan pressed him, "Even if it is the will of God?"

"If it were the will of God, He would find His own means, and maybe that is what He did. We are humble servants of God, but we follow His will as laid down in the holy scriptures. We do not make it up according to our convenience. We leave that to the Catholics and the Jews."

I sighed. "Do you know Greg Carson?"

He nodded. "He was a friend of our sons. His father was a good man."

"Do you have much contact with him?"

"No, Detective. We don't have much contact with anyone. We work, we tend our simple plot of land, and we serve God in whatever ways we can each day, and give thanks for his mercy. We don't socialize, we see few people from one month to the next."

I'd heard everything I needed to hear, and about as much as I was willing to. I looked across the table at Dehan. She gave her head a shake and I stood.

"We won't take up any more of your time." They didn't get up with us but stayed sitting at the table as we made our way to the door. I opened it for Dehan and then turned back to look at them, both staring down at the simple, plain tabletop their God had blessed them with.

"Do you know your Bible, Mr. Olvera? How about you, Mrs. Olvera? You know your Bible?"

He answered for them both. "We are rigorous in our Bible study, Detective."

"You familiar with Matthew?" They both looked away. I insisted, "Matthew 7:1, Judge not, that ye be not judged. Matthew 7:2, For with what judgment ye judge, ye shall be judged: and with what measure ye mete, it shall be measured to you again. Matthew 7:3, And why beholdest thou the mote that is in thy brother's eye, but considerest not the beam that is in thine own eye?" I gave my head a little sideways twist. "You sure you don't 'make it up according to your own convenience'? A good day to you both."

We left them in their simple, plain house, probably judging us and sentencing us to eternal damnation, and strolled through the broad, empty streets of Seven Hills back toward the Wagon Wheel. After a bit, Dehan said, "You memorized the *Bible*?"

"No, I just happened to Google that quote the other day, for something unrelated." I shrugged. "Synchronicity."

She said absently, "A Jungian concept." I raised an eyebrow at her. She looked defiant. "What? I Google too." She looked away and stuck her hands in her pockets. "So maybe they are religious fanatics. Maybe they hate the Vuolo girls for taking their sons away. Maybe she called . . ."

"They have no phone."

"Okay, so maybe she wrote them and they said, 'Yeah, come up, we'll talk about it.' Papa Freak met her at the station, drove her up to Lefthand Canyon, badabim badabam, end of story." She curled her lip and shook her head. "But I don't think so. I can't tell you why, I just don't get that vibe from them."

"Vibe . . . Cosmic vibrations aside, I can't see Kathleen ever *wanting* to go and visit them. Especially if she was depressed. It's extremely improbable. And if there ever was any correspondence between them, it's going to be damned hard to prove, because there will be no electronic record of it."

She nodded. "I agree. Greg is our guy." I smiled. She eyed me. "What?"

"Go back to the kitchen and make the tea, woman."

"Can you believe that? What keeps a woman with a guy like that?"

We walked in silence and I studied the cold, empty blue sky above us. "I think some people stick together just because they're terrified of someday dying alone." I frowned at her. She was watching me with an odd, quizzical expression. I said, "Dying alone is a pretty scary thought."

She made a kind of "pffff" sound and looked away. "Crazy, isn't it? People will live all their lives alone, even when they are close to somebody. I mean, they won't *commit*—take that step and *commit*. But what scares them is dying alone. You know? I don't mind spending my whole, goddamn life alone, as long as I don't *die* alone!"

We walked in silence to the car and got in.

NINE

WE FOLLOWED THE SAME ROUTE WE'D FOLLOWED THAT morning, winding between the steep, densely forested slopes, till eventually we came to Gold Hill. Gold Hill has four streets: Main Street, Gold Run Street, Suicide Hill Street, and the fourth street has no name. These are intersected by Prospect Street and a couple of others which also have no names. None of these streets is tarmacadamed, and there are no traffic lights or stop signs. And all the houses have plenty of space between them, so they can stretch and expand with gardens, orchards, and vegetable patches. As we rolled slowly through the town along Main Street, it made me smile. I thought it would be a good place to be a kid in. I imagined how it must have seemed to the young Kathleen and Pat, accustomed to the crowds and restrictions of the Bronx, to experience this wild freedom. What it must have been like when they first came to visit Greg at the ranch.

We followed the sheriff's directions and soon came out the other side of town. The road forked, and there was a rough sign that told us this was Pine Ranch. We turned in and followed the drive to a large, two-story, log-built house with a raised porch. I pulled up there, climbed out, and leaned on the roof of the car, looking at the land around. There was a lot of it, and I could see cattle, llamas, and lots of wood. Whatever Greg was, he wasn't poor.

The door opened as Dehan got out, and a man stepped onto the porch. He looked lean and tough. He was tall, about thirty-two, good-looking, and dressed in boots and a cowboy hat. He looked the part. He eyed us both without warmth and said, "Help you?"

"Are you Greg Carson?"

"Who's asking?"

"This is Detective Dehan and I am Detective Stone. We are collaborating with the Lee County Sheriff's Department . . ."

"You here about Kathleen?"

"Yes."

"You can put your badge away. I don't need to see it. Tom Watson said you'd be coming. There ain't a lot I can tell you." He came down the steps. "What do you want to know?"

Dehan said, "Did she tell you she was coming to Seven Hills?"

"Nope."

"She wasn't in touch with you in the weeks before her death?"

"Nope."

I smiled and came around the car to stand in front of him. "Mr. Carson, I should tell you that we have requested Kathleen's phone records, emails, and social media records for June and July of that year. If you were in touch with her, we will see the correspondence."

He gave me a long, level, hard look. "I just got through telling you we didn't have any contact. Do I have to repeat it?"

"When was the last time you did have contact with her?"

He took a deep breath and looked out at the horizon. "Must have been 2010, 2009? Thereabouts. After her an' Mo got hitched I didn't really see much of them."

Dehan raised an eyebrow. "Why was that?"

He shrugged and grinned. "I guess I always liked Kath myself. After her pa died, that little weasel Mo was in there like greased lightning. They used to come up regular in the summer, and each summer I hoped maybe she'd've got over him. But she didn't. She still liked him. After a couple of years, I just gave up." He gave her a humorless once-over and added, "I don't like wasting time."

I asked, "Were you aware that she and Mo were having difficulties in their marriage?"

"How would I know that?"

"Can you answer the question, please, Mr. Carson?"

"Nope." He let the ambiguity of his answer stand.

"Did you know she was coming to visit?"

"I already told you I didn't."

I nodded. "Here's my problem, Mr. Carson. We know for a fact that Kathleen left New York and came to Seven Hills. We know for a fact that she was coming here to see somebody. We are almost certain that that somebody picked her up from the train station in Boulder . . ."

He shook his head. "No, they didn't."

"They didn't? How do you know that?"

"The train don't go to Boulder. You want to come to Boulder from New York by train, you're gonna get the train to Denver, and then a bus from Denver to Downtown Boulder Station, on Fourteenth Street."

There was amusement in his face. I let him finish and smiled. "Thank you. So we know almost for a certainty that somebody picked her up from Downtown Boulder Bus Station. And that was probably the last person to see her alive. Now, there are only three people that she would have told that she was coming. Her in-laws, and you. And we know it wasn't her in-laws."

He looked down at the ground and nodded a few times. Finally he said, "You're right."

"You did pick her up from the bus station?"

"Nope. You're right that you got a problem."

Dehan sighed. "Can you think of anybody else that she might have been in touch with, that she might have been coming to see?"

He took off his hat and scratched his head with the same

hand. He seemed to think about it. "Pat was a bit wild. She made friends with the off-grid crowd. Some of them farm cannabis and hang out with Hells Angels. They meet at the Shack."

"The Shack?"

"It's a bar down on Lefthand Canyon, 'bout three or four mile east of here, before the bend. They have themselves some pretty wild parties down there. I won't say I never been. I went once or twice with Pat. But that ain't my scene."

I scratched my head in an unconscious echo of his own gesture. "So would Kathleen have had friends in that crowd?"

"I can't see it m'self, but I don't know. And to be honest, you're wasting my time. I got work to do and I told you everything I know."

I nodded. "I understand. Thanks for talking to us, Mr. Carson." I moved toward the car, then stopped and turned back. "You didn't like Kathleen, did you?"

He lifted his chin and gave me a hard stare. "I didn't say that. I told you I was sweet on her at one time."

"You didn't say it, but you didn't have to. It's clear you don't give a damn that she's dead. The five of you used to hang out when you were kids and in your teens, you say you were sweet on her, but now she's been murdered, and you can't spare ten lousy minutes to help the cops find her killer? You had a grudge." I shook my head. "You had some reason for turning hostile against a girl everybody else describes as an angel. What happened, Greg?" He didn't answer. I pointed at him. "You're still my man for picking her up at the station." I smiled. "Have a good day, and thanks for your valuable time. You've been helpful."

We climbed back in the car and slammed the doors. Dehan muttered, "Prick," and I fired up the engine. I saw him in the rearview mirror, watching us as we pulled out of the ranch.

We rolled slowly back through the town, and I turned left onto Lickskillet Road. We bumped and bounced down the track till we came to Lefthand Canyon Drive, where I turned left and drove slowly, among the growing shadows on the hills and the pine woods, for about four miles. Just before the road turned north, I saw a ramshackle building on the left, set back about thirty yards, half in among the trees. It was made mainly of wood, with a tall, rickety, gray stone chimney that ran all the way down to the ground on the right-hand wall. There was a broad porch at the front and an open garden, where you could see all the ground had been churned up, and the grass and weeds crushed, by vehicles entering and leaving. I pulled over and climbed out to have a look. There were shutters closed over the windows, and when I tried the door, it was locked. I walked down the side and put my hand on the stone chimney. It was cold.

As I came back to the garden, Dehan was approaching from the other side. She shook her head. "Nothing. You think this is it?"

I shrugged with my eyebrows. "It looks like a shack, and it's where he said it would be." I didn't say anything for a moment, looking around, listening. It was real quiet. You could feel the evening gathering, and even the birds were silent. I asked, "You think there's anything in it?"

She made a face. "Kathleen as a dope smoker? Not really."

"How about Kathleen coming to her sister's rescue?"

"Oh man . . ."

I rested my ass on the trunk of the car and stared at the old ramshackle building.

"What we still haven't got, Dehan, is a concrete reason why she came here, *or* why she lied about where she was going. Let me rephrase that. We don't know *where* she was going, what her purpose was in going there, or what made her lie about it. All we have is that she lied to her mother and her husband about going to see Ingrid and Alfredo, and she turned up a week later, ten miles away from their house, beheaded, ill-concealed in the woods."

Dehan sighed and ran her fingers through her thick hair. "So, how would that work? Her sister gets in with bad company. Cannabis is legal in Colorado, but it's not in New York. Maybe they had a bit of business going, with Pat selling the produce back east. She gets into trouble with them. Who knows? Maybe they were giving her merchandise to sell and she kept the proceeds, didn't pay, spent it on coke—whatever. They want their money. They're going to come to New York to collect. She convinces Kathleen to come to the Shack and pay them off, plead for time—again, whatever. Point is, they are mad, and they make an example of her."

"It's plausible. It's no less plausible than Greg raping her. We need to come back when they're open."

She nodded. "Maybe your man Ned knows what their hours are."

I smiled. "You think?"

"You never can tell with these clean-living, God fearin' country folk, Stone. They often have dark secrets."

The sun slipped behind the trees. Suddenly, there was a sharp chill in the air and the sky seemed to darken. I shifted my ass off the trunk and moved toward the driver's side.

"You know what they have here, Dehan, as well as bull's balls?"

"What's that, Stone?"

"Bison steak." I climbed in and slammed the door. Dehan got in beside me. I fired up the engine and she turned on the heater. "You ever had a bison steak, Dehan?"

"Nope, but I reckon bison steak is something I could get pretty intense about. I propose a shower, a craft beer followed by a bottle of good wine, and a couple of bison steaks. I think that might be mighty helpful in stimulatin' them there gray cells."

"Well, I's inclined to agree, ma'am, bein' partial to a beer an' a bison steak myself."

And we drove off, into the sunset.

TEN

THEY HAD PULLED THE DRAPES IN THE DINING ROOM and built up the fire. It was agreeably warm and, looking across the table at Dehan, who was holding her beer and gazing at the burning logs, it was easy to forget we were working and to imagine we were on holiday. I was vaguely surprised that the idea of being on holiday with Dehan did not strike me as odd.

She took a deep breath and frowned. "Here's the way my mind is working, Stone. Our suspect pool is small." She dragged her gaze away from the burning logs and looked at me. "We have an unknown possible at the Shack, or we have Greg. Whichever way you turn it, we end up with the same result." She raised her shoulders. "I just can't imagine that we are going to come up with another suspect. It's either Mr. X, or it's Greg."

I dragged my mind back from the strange places where it had been wandering and thought about what she had said.

"I agree."

"So we need to eliminate either Mr. X or Greg."

"Getting hold of her credit card, phone records, and emails will help."

She grunted quietly and turned back to the fire. "There is not a lot more we can do with Greg right now until we get those records . . ."

I interrupted her. "Actually, there may be."

She frowned. "Like what?"

"The DNA samples taken with the rape kit. DNA testing has come on since 2012. I think we should resubmit the semen, have it sent to Frank back at the lab, see if he can make anything of it."

She nodded. "Yeah, that's good."

"It will be interesting to see how Greg reacts when we ask him for a sample for comparison."

"Yeah." She nodded again. "Anyway, where was I going . . . I've been thinking about the Shack." She grinned. "According to Ned, they open after nine p.m., and it's 'not the sort of place we would want to go.' If we turn up there looking like this . . ." She gestured across the table at me with her open hand, then back at herself with both hands. "Let's face it, we have 'COPS' written all over us. Not only will they not tell us shit, we'll be lucky to get out alive."

I frowned. "What do you suggest?"

"We don't go as cops."

"Undercover?"

"Not exactly. I don't think we are authorized to conduct an undercover investigation here, so there could be problems with the legality of any evidence we gather that way. But there is nothing to stop us going along for a drink, is there?" She spread her hands. "We're waiting on Kathleen's records, we have some time to kill, we heard there's a bar of local interest, so we went along in our free time . . ."

I smiled. "We don't need to tell them we're cops."

She grinned again. "And if we are off duty, we don't need to *look* like cops."

Peaches and Cream's mother brought out our bison steaks with a look of real satisfaction on her face, like she'd bred them, slaughtered them, and cooked them herself. She poured the wine and said, "Enjoy your meal," as though she really meant it. We did our best.

The next twenty minutes went by in almost total silence. If you have never eaten a bison steak, it is hard to convey just how engrossing they can be. These animals live wild, they eat grass, and they are not pumped full of hormones and other crap. The meat is lean and has a flavor that is hard to describe, except to say that it is beyond exquisite. In Valhalla, only Odin gets to eat bison steak. It would not be an exaggeration to say that we ate in reverent silence. The only sound that we were aware of was the crackle and spit of the fire. Occasionally we would pause to sip the wine and exchange a smile. Other than that, we focused only on the noble meat.

When the last piece was gone, we sat back in our chairs and Dehan drained her glass.

"Man," she said, and nodded slowly.

"What did I tell you? Is that something?"

I called Peaches and Cream Sr. over and ordered a Bushmills, and Dehan had one too. Then we sat with our chairs turned toward the fire and our legs stretched out and sipped.

"Don't shave."

"Okay."

"And after you shower in the morning, don't brush your hair, just let it dry anyhow. We'll get you a sweatshirt from the general store, and some jeans, and maybe some Timberland boots. Get you roughed up a bit."

"What about you?"

"I look rough anyhow. Maybe I'll get a woolen hat, and some of those gloves with no fingers. You know the ones?"

"Uh-huh."

"You know how to roll a cigarette?"

"No."

"Okay, I'll roll them for you."

"I don't smoke."

"You did once, and you will again tomorrow night."

I studied her face. She was smirking at the fire. She was right, though. If we were going to get any information from the crowd at the Shack, we needed to fit in, and that meant being a couple of dopeheads from New York looking for some fun in Colorado. I sighed.

"But we go armed."

"Yup."

"And let's be clear about our objective."

She nodded. "You want to define it for us?"

I thought about it. "We are there to find out, A, if they had a deal with Pat to distribute and/or sell dope in New York, and B, if Kathleen came to see them on the night of . . ." I thought about it. It was a forty-hour journey at least. "On the night of the eighth of July."

"Agreed." She sipped her whiskey and rolled it around her mouth for a moment before swallowing it and sighing. "Man, that's good. So, we're going to have to play it by ear, but we should have some kind of basic plan."

"Yeah, I would say our main target is the barkeep. Try and get into conversation with him. Maybe we are open to doing some business with him, selling dope back in the Big Apple. See where that leads us. Meanwhile, sound out the other customers too, see if anybody remembers either of them."

"And if they get suspicious . . ."

"We leave. We don't want a conflict on Sheriff Watson's turf. And we sure as hell don't want a shoot-out."

We were quiet for a while. With the wine and the whiskey, and the warmth of the fire, I was finding it hard to keep my mind on the case. Dehan seemed to be miles away, transfixed by the wavering flames. The orange light bathed her face and I was struck, not for the first time, by how perfect her features were. It was a fact she seemed to be totally unaware of. I surprised myself by asking, "How are things with your Uncle Ben? He still trying to fix you up with rich surgeons?"

She gave a small, comfortable laugh. "No, I behaved so badly with the last surgeon he tried to set me up with, I think he's given me up as a lost cause." She sipped and sighed again. "You ever miss it? Family life?"

I hesitated, not sure what the answer was. "I miss the idea of it. The idea of the companionship. The idea of being able to share a thought, an idea, a feeling, without having to say anything." I shrugged. "But I never had that. How can you miss something you never had?"

She looked at me for a long moment. Her expression was serious. Eventually she said, "I don't know. But I miss it too, and I never had it either." She drained her glass and leaned forward to slap my leg. "C'mon, big guy. Let's get some sleep." She stood. "If you snore, I'll gut you and leave your body in Lefthand Canyon for the coyotes."

"Snore?" I said, as we tramped up the stairs. "The way you hawk and stridulate, I'll be lucky to get to sleep at all."

"*Hawk and stridulate . . . ?*"

"Yup."

THE NEXT DAY was pretty uneventful. I was not allowed to shave when I got up, and after I showered, Dehan spent almost fifteen minutes jabbing her fingers through my hair to make it look as though I hadn't combed it. Apparently, if I simply didn't comb it, it looked as though I had combed it. That's forty-six wasted years right there.

Then, after breakfast, we went and spent three hundred bucks on buying clothes to make me look disreputable: some torn jeans that were more expensive than the ones that hadn't got torn yet, a black sweatshirt with a large cannabis leaf on it and the legend, "High, how'ya doin?" in faded letters, and a pair of Timberland boots that cost almost as much as my car.

This all made Dehan smile a lot. "Yeah, man. You look cool. You should dress down a bit, you know that?"

"What is this, Dehan? Is this method? Are you getting into your role for tonight?"

She raised an eyebrow at me, which made the manager of the general store simper and move away to his till. "Hey, dude, I don't know where you were raised, Stone. But I was raised on the mean streets of the Bronx. I don't need no method. I *am* the streets!"

I rolled my eyes and paid, and we took my new image to trudge through the woods in Lefthand Canyon for a few hours till the sun started to slip. We found nothing, but that was pretty much what we expected to find. Five years of snow, rain, wind, large and small animals, and a million bugs had removed any trace of Kathleen's murder and her killer. Nature is ruthless about life and death. They are to her as breathing in and out are to us. It's only human beings who make a big deal out of it.

As the sun began to slide off the big blue dome of the sky and into the western hills, we began to trudge, slide, and stumble down the steep bank toward my car. Then Dehan stuck her hands in her back pockets and asked, "So, Stone, I'm a working-class girl from the Bronx, Mexican Catholic mom, Jewish dad. You know all this about me. What about you? You're pretty secretive, you know. Stone . . ." She savored the name. "What is that? English? German? You working class? Middle class?" She spread her hands. "You drive a classic Jaguar. You know your wines. You use words like 'stridulate.' What's the deal with you?"

We got to the bottom of the hill and came out of the woods and I unlocked the car. We climbed in, and I sat for a while staring at the road as dusk slowly encroached. Finally, I shrugged.

"No deal. I'm not secretive, there's just not much to tell. Your family is more interesting than mine. Dad traced his family back to the War of Independence. They were Anglo-Saxon Protestants. Brooklyn. Strict, strong. Fought for the king." I laughed without much feeling. "Always defending the losing side, that's us. Mom was a small, pretty, weak woman. They were unhappy, but never enough to talk about it, and never enough to do anything to fix it." I smiled at her. "They did their duty, and then they died."

"Wow . . ."

"Not really. No big deal."

I turned the key, felt the satisfying rumble of the big four-liter engine, and pulled away, back toward Gold Hill. Dehan shifted in her seat so she could face me.

"I remember something I read once about Chagall."

I raised my eyebrows. "Chagall, the painter?"

"Yeah. I told you. You're not the only guy who uses Google, remember? It said that the important thing about Chagall was not what he put into his paintings, but everything that he left out."

"Huh."

"I didn't get it at the time, but now I understand what they meant. It's what you just did."

"Is it?"

"You know it is. You just told me exactly nothing about your childhood and your family. But when you did that, you told me everything."

We ground and bumped our way up Lickskillet Road and then headed east back toward Seven Hills. Eventually, as we were approaching the Wagon Wheel, I said, "So, we going for another bison steak tonight, before the Shack, or something lighter?"

She looked at me a long time before answering. Finally, she said, "I don't do light, Stone. I do heavy, and intense. It's part of the stereotype. Like you with your WASP stiff upper lip."

ELEVEN

We arrived at the Shack at ten. The shutters were open and the windows were glowing with a warm, amber light that turned the building and the hillside behind it into a black mass against the translucent night sky. It reflected off the chassis of a handful of trucks and bikes, and occasionally flickered as a body moved past inside. You could make out the strains of music. It sounded like the Eagles. Some things never die.

I parked near the gate, where I couldn't be blocked in, and where it would be easy to get out in a hurry if we needed to. Dehan gave my hair a last ruffle and we climbed out into the icy night air.

We pushed through the old wooden door into a surprisingly large, crowded room. There was no hush as we stepped in. They didn't all go quiet and turn to look at us with suspicious eyes. They ignored us completely.

On the far right, there was a large, stone, open fireplace built up with big logs. It was burning well, casting an agreeable, flickering glow, and the room was warm. There were maybe fifteen tables scattered around the floor, and most of them were occupied. On the left, opposite the fire, there was a long bar with two men behind it, serving drinks to half a dozen guys leaning on the counter. At a couple of tables in the corner, by the fire, I counted six men in biker's leathers. They were all either bald or had very long hair. A couple of them had forked beards. On their jackets they bore the emblem of the local chapter of the Hells Angels.

Just about everybody else looked like your stereotypical off-grid hippie, in used jeans, nondescript shirts, and long hair. About the only thing to distinguish the men from the women was that most of the women didn't have beards, and most of the men didn't have breasts. Most.

The only people who stood out from the crowd were two guys who were sitting with the Angels in the corner. If they'd been in a club in the Bronx I wouldn't even have noticed them. Here they stood out like nuns at a clip joint. One of them looked like Ray Charles, black glasses and all. He laughed a lot and held a cigarette in his left hand in a way that told you he was never without it.

Next to him was a Latino in his mid or late thirties. He had pale blue eyes you could see clean across the room, and a scar down his left cheek that twisted his mouth and made it look as though everything he looked at he found nauseating.

I saw all this in the time it takes to close a door. Then Dehan was clinging to my arm and leaning on me and saying, "Stop staring, laugh and buy me a drink."

She laughed to illustrate her point and pulled me toward the bar. We found a vacant spot and one of the barmen approached us, smiling.

"Hey! New faces. Good to see, man. I'm Saul." He held out his hand and we shook. He didn't sound like a cowboy. He was East Coast.

I took his hand. "I'm John."

"Carmen. I *love* this place!"

He laughed. "Cute, huh? What can I get you?"

"Couple of beers." He went away to get them from the fridge and I looked at Dehan. "Not what I expected."

She nodded. "We need to talk to the guys in the corner."

Saul came back with our drinks. "You need glasses?"

I shook my head and grinned at him. "You're from back east, right?"

He laughed. "Same as you, pal. New York." He grabbed a cloth and gave the bar a wipe. He looked ready to chat for a bit.

"How'd you wind up here, if you don't mind me asking?"

He made a face like acquired wisdom and laughed. "Senior year at NYU, law. And one morning I woke up, literally. You know what I'm saying? And I made a long movie in my head, about where the law was taking me. The firm, the two cars, the mortgage, the wife, the affairs—the whole damned script had been written for me by The System before I was even born." He shook his head. Then he laughed and shrugged. "Only I didn't want to be a part of that movie. So I upset my mom and my dad, borrowed some money from the bank against my inheritance, and bought this place. And that's my story."

Dehan looked at him with wonder in her eyes. For a moment I asked myself if it was an act or genuine. "Wow, that is so cool."

"Anyone can do it, sister. Happiness is a choice, right? How about you guys, what are you doing up here?"

Before I could answer, Dehan grabbed my arm with both of hers and leaned her head on my shoulder. "We are kind of doing something similar, right, honey? We're making a long movie. We want to get out of the race, and we're looking at cool places. We don't want to go totally off-grid, but we want to be somewhere where you can see the stars at night, and maybe grow some weed without The Man watching you. Know what I mean?" She managed to say it all and sound authentic. He nodded. "So we were thinking of Arizona. But we met this chick and she said, 'Go to Colorado.' And she told us about the Shack."

His face lit up. "No kidding? What's her name?"

She rested her chin on my shoulder a couple of inches from my face and gazed adoringly into my eyes. "What was her name, John?"

I sighed, like I was thinking. "Uh, Pat."

He frowned. "Oh, Irish kid?"

I made a face. "Yeah, she could be Irish."

He nodded. "I remember her. She used to hang out here with a big cowboy type. Haven't seen either of them for a while." He nodded over at Ray Charles. "Sly and Coy knew her. She was part of their crowd."

Dehan laughed. "Sly and Coy?"

He chuckled. "Sylvester is the blind black guy. Coy says he's Mexican and back home they called him 'El Coyote' on account of how badass he was. But everybody up here is badass, except the refugees from the city, like me. They called him Coy and it stuck, so now he has to live with it. Personally I call him Coyote, just to be on the safe side, know what I'm saying?"

I made scared eyes and said, "Okay."

He walked away and started serving other customers. Dehan swigged from her bottle. "We need to make a move."

I nodded and smiled like she'd said something amusing. "I know. But give it a while. If we're too quick it will look suspicious."

We talked about nothing much through "Tequila Sunrise" and "Desperado" and finished our beers. I called Saul over.

"Let's have another couple of beers, Saul. Will you have one too?"

"Thank you kindly!"

He went to get them, and when he returned, I said, "Listen, you been here long?"

"Coming up for ten years."

"Maybe you can give us some advice."

"If I can, I will. Always happy to help. Cheers!"

We knocked bottles and drank. I sighed through my teeth and said, "We're looking to do a bit of business."

He raised an eyebrow. He knew what was coming, but he asked anyway. "What kind of business?"

I spread my hands and smiled on the right side of my face, acknowledging it was obvious. "Weed is legal up here but, as I am sure you know, it's not back in New York. So if I sell it back there I can ask a good price . . ."

"You want to know if there is a cannabis farmer who is willing to sell you in bulk so you can sell it in the city."

I shrugged like it wasn't a big deal. "You know—it's one of the options we're looking at."

He gave me a wink. "Let me have a word with Sly. I don't get involved in that shit. I keep my nose clean. But I know they have done that in the past. Give me a minute. Just don't get me involved."

I thanked him and he went away. Dehan took a pull from her bottle. "So Sly and El Coyote are farmers. But they sure as hell aren't farming for the pharmaceutical industry. They are supplying the states where dope is still illegal, and they can make top dollar on an ounce." She looked worried. "You ever smoked dope, Stone?"

I shrugged. "Couple of times at college. I thought it was over-rated. Why?" She gave me a look that was hard to interpret. Then it dawned on me. "You never did." She shook her head. "And you think we're going to have to tonight." She nodded.

I looked over at Saul speaking in Sly's ear. Coy and a couple of the Angels glanced over at us. I was beginning to think this was a bad idea and said so to Dehan. She made a "maybe" face. "It's too late now, anyway. We'll have to talk to them."

"We can't get stoned. It's crazy."

"What's it like? Is it like getting drunk?"

I closed my eyes. A voice in my head said we should leave. Now. I said, "Not really. I thought it was kind of boring. It hits you suddenly. Everything seems real funny or real deep. Some-times you lose your inhibitions. It can be an aphrodisiac. This is really a bad idea, Dehan, we should go."

She gave me a weird kind of blank grin that was impossible to interpret, and Saul approached us behind the bar.

"You're in luck. He wants you to join him for a drink. He

seems to be interested. If he offers you a smoke, accept. It's damn good weed, and he's easily offended."

I grinned at him. "Don't worry. We'll accept! Say, bring us over a bottle of good tequila, will you? As a goodwill gesture."

He winked. "That's nice. He'll like that."

As we made to move to Sly's table, I put my hand on Dehan's shoulder and reached for my phone. I made like I was answering a call. She watched me. As I hung up, I set the alarm for twenty minutes and put it back in my pocket.

"Okay, Carmen. Into the jaws of the coyote. Let's go."

TWELVE

THERE WERE SIX OF THEM AROUND THE TABLE: SLY IN the corner with Coy on his right, and a chorus of four Angels around him. I put a smile of invincible middle-class naïvety on my face, and we walked over at the same time Saul arrived with a tray of tequila and eight glasses. We'd reached Hotel California on the Eagles' Greatest Hits.

"Good evening."

I smiled around the table as Saul set down the bottle and the glasses with a saucer of lemon slices and a salt cellar. They all looked at me without expression, and then at Dehan with more approval. Saul said to Sly, "Bottle of tequila, compliments of John here, Sly."

Sly cocked his head and smiled. "That is a nice gesture you had there, John. But before I invite you to sit at my table and join me and my family here"—he made a broad, elegant gesture around the table—"let me tell you something that I have learned in life. I have learned that no man ever gives anything to another man unless he wants something in return. Would you say that is true, John?"

I allowed my smile to turn from naïve to rueful. "Well, it is certainly true in my case, Sly."

He gave a high-pitched, wheezing laugh that was chock-full of the pleasure of being right. "Well, at least you is honest, my man. As you might perceive, I am blind, but that don't mean I don't see, does it now?"

"Clearly not."

"Sit down, you and your friend, who I am told is *hot*, and tell me what it is you want from me. And I shall tell you whether I shall grant it to you, or send you on your way. Move over, boys, and make room for our guests."

There was some shifting and scraping of chairs and we sat on Sly's left. Every seeing eye in the company was fixed on Dehan. Their expressions were appreciative, but not exactly complimentary. I felt edgy but tried to hide it.

"Well," I said. "Aside from the pleasure of your hospitality, we are looking to do some business in Colorado, and we were thinking you might be the man to do business with, or you might know somebody."

There was something serpentine about his smile and his voice. "What kind of business, John?"

"We are looking to buy good-quality weed in fair quantities and sell it back in New York. It could be profitable to all, while only we would shoulder any risk."

His face became serious. "What you are proposing is illegal."

I allowed the smile to show in my voice. "Only half of what I am proposing is illegal. And that half doesn't concern you, except in that you would receive a higher price than if it were *entirely* legal."

He raised an eyebrow, and I could visualize his sightless eyes behind the black lenses of his shades. "Do I look like a criminal to you?"

He was trying to intimidate me, and I am not good at being intimidated. My answer probably wasn't wise, but my edginess was turning to anger, and I was finding it increasingly hard to hide it. I looked him over, and then around at the company. I shrugged and said, "Yeah, you do."

There was a moment of tension and I was half hoping they'd get mad. Instead, Sly started laughing. "You might be a dumb motherfucker, John, but you sure as hell got balls. I'll give you that."

"Impressions can be deceiving, Sly. I'm not as dumb as I look. How about we operate on a footing of mutual respect and see if we can do business? Straight off, I can distribute throughout the Bronx. I have friends in the Sureños whom I can work with and who will safeguard the territory."

"Oh man, that is big talk. You telling me the Sureños ain't got a supplier already?"

"No. I am not telling you that. I am telling you that they can use another supplier and that their current supplier hasn't got the quality or the quantity I figure I can get from you."

"Is that so . . . ?" It didn't seem worth answering, so I waited. Finally, he asked, "How much?"

"How about we start with ten kilos. Can you supply that much?"

He wheezed his high-pitched laugh and everybody joined in. "Oh, I can supply that much, and much more. The question is, can you provide the money for that much dope?"

"That depends on what price you're looking for."

"How much you willing to pay?"

Dehan spoke suddenly, and there was an edge to her voice. "How much was Pat paying? We'll pay the same."

Everybody went very still. Sly tilted his head to one side. Coy stared at her with his nasty, pale blue eyes. Sly said, "Excuse me?"

"Let's cut the crap, Sly. We're here because of Pat. She said you could supply us. We'll deal on the same terms you had with her."

He turned to Coy, leaned close to his ear, and muttered something. Coy didn't remove his eyes from Dehan. He muttered something back and Sly nodded.

"We haven't seen Pat for . . . oh, five or six years. What makes you think I had any kind of deal with her?"

Dehan snapped, "She does. She didn't mention you by name, but she said she had a supplier in the Shack. So we came here. I figure she was talking about you. Unless there's somebody else we should be talking to. You got a problem with Pat?"

"Is that any of your business?"

I was about to intercede when Dehan said, "Yeah. It's my business. She recommended you, and you seem to have a problem with that. I want to buy weed from you. So yeah, if you have a problem with her, that's my business, because I don't want to have the same problem as her. That make sense to you, Sly? Coz it makes sense to me."

There was absolute stillness at the table. In my mind I was already reaching for my piece. Dehan was completely unfazed. She looked around the table and gestured at the bottle of tequila. "Are we going to just sit here and look at this mother or are we going to drink it?"

Sly threw back his head and let out a loud whoop. "*Man!* I do like a strong woman. You like black meat, baby? Coz I sure as hell am into you."

I spoke without thinking and the aggression in my voice surprised even me. "She's my wife. Back off."

He raised both hands and laughed. Dehan's eyes went wide. Sly said, "Okay, my man, take it easy. No offense. You don't know 'less you ask, am I right? Open up the bottle, Coyote. Let's drink."

Dehan glanced at me and smiled. We had a round of shots and I broached the subject again. "Carmen's right, Sly. If you have a problem with Pat, we need to know. We don't want to tread on your toes or cause any offense. She told us about the Shack, but she didn't mention any names."

He let out a long sigh and reached in a woven bag he had hung around his neck. He pulled out a tin of buds, some papers, and a grinder, and started preparing a long joint.

"Pat . . ." he said. "Pat, Pat, Pat . . . She used to hang out with that cowboy dude. She had a pretty sister. Am I right?"

I shrugged. "I have no idea."

"All the guys liked her sister. She never came here, you understand. Her sister was a nice Catholic girl." He made an obscene noise in his throat that turned into a laugh. "Catholic girls. My favorite!"

He rolled the joint with long, skillful fingers and sealed it with a long tongue. He poked it in his mouth and lit it with a match, then inhaled deeply and held it down for five long seconds before exhaling. He spoke as he exhaled.

"I have no problem with Pat. She was nothing to me. I sold her dope, you understand, and she did not always pay on time. But we sorted it out amicably." He leered at me. "Like I say, I *love* Catholic girls."

He threw his head back and laughed out loud. When the laugh had subsided, he handed me the joint. I took a drag, pretended to inhale and hold it down, counted to four, and exhaled slowly through my nose. Then I passed it to Dehan. She took a drag and I turned to Sly.

"I'll give you two and a half grand a kilo. That's thirty grand for the first lot of ten K."

He giggled. "I know how much you're going to sell it for, man . . ."

Dehan erupted into a fit of coughing and everybody at the table started laughing. I turned to her and saw her eyes were streaming. "Oh, man . . ." She took another drag and passed it to the biker next to her, a giant with a forked beard who was watching her with hungry eyes.

I turned back to Sly. "I sell it to my contact in the Sureños. *They* get the market price. Two and a half K is my offer."

The joint made another round. I looked at Dehan. Her pupils were dilated but she said, "I'm okay."

Sly's voice rose above the music and the noise of talk and laughter. "Agreed, John. We can do business. I can have it for you in . . . a couple of days, Coyote?"

"Two days."

"Two days. So, let's celebrate."

Coy refilled the glasses and Sly started rolling another joint. Dehan was smiling at me. I was wondering if my damned alarm was ever going to go off. Sly took a long drag on his joint, lay back in his chair, and let out the smoke real slow. While he did it, he handed me the cigarette. I took a drag, held it in my mouth for a count of three, and let it out again. I handed it to Dehan, willing her to do the same. She looked slightly worried.

She took a drag, inhaled and held it down, suppressing a coughing fit, then let it out and passed the butt to the big Angel.

My phone rang. I took it out of my pocket and looked at the screen. I turned to Sly. "Excuse me. I have to take this."

I stood and moved away a couple of steps, saying, "Yuh . . . uh-huh . . . okay . . ."

The big Angel was leaning over close to Dehan, with his arm across the back of her chair. I felt a hot pellet in my belly. I wasn't sure if it was anger, fear, or a volatile mixture of the two. I put my phone away and returned to the table.

"Sorry to break up the party, folks. We have to go."

Dehan looked up at me. Her expression was grateful. The Angel, not so much. He looked resentful. He said, "The lady don't need to go. You can go, she can stay."

I smiled amiably. "The lady needs to go too."

I reached out to her and she took my hand. She made to get to her feet, but he put his hand on her shoulder and forced her down. Any other time that would have cost him a broken arm. But the dope was kicking in and mixing with the tequila and the beer, plus the wine we'd had with dinner. She dropped back into the chair and looked at me in alarm.

I said, "Take your hand off my wife."

"How's about you make me, boy?"

I turned to Sly and Coy. "This how you do business?"

Coy looked at the Angel and shook his head. "Leave it, Scott."

I pulled Dehan to her feet and looked back at Coy. His pale eyes were real cold. "Nice doing business with you."

I put my arm around Dehan and guided her to the door, then out into the icy night air. She shuddered. Our steps were loud on the dirt as we crossed to the car. I unlocked the passenger door and opened it. It had to happen, and it did. His voice stopped us and echoed across the lot.

"Hey, boy, don't run away. Let's talk."

I said to Dehan, "Get in. Can you drive?"

She shook her head and leaned against the car. "I need a minute."

But I could see from her eyes it was going to take a lot more than a minute. I turned. It was Scott and two of his pals.

"What do you want?"

"You know what I want, boy. And I want it right here and now, so you can watch." He laughed. "Don't worry. I won't hurt her. She's gonna love it. Can't speak for my boys here, though. *They* might hurt her, a bit."

I smiled. "You're pretty tough, huh? You tough enough to come here and get her without the help of your nanny goats there?"

He was laughing. He turned to his pals with a mock Texas accent. "Hold my beer, boys. We gonna party."

I heard Dehan whisper behind me. "Stone, don't . . ."

He was strong, but he had a big belly and he was drunk. He took two running strides at me, swinging a huge right cross. If it had connected, it would have taken my head off. But he was as slow as a sloth on Prozac. I stepped in and easily blocked the punch with my left while I simultaneously drove my right down onto his belly, putting all my two hundred and twenty pounds behind it. His eyes bulged and his tongue stuck out. His cheeks flushed purple, and he made a horrible, wheezing, choking sound.

He staggered back a bit, but it wasn't enough to get him away from the three venomous crosses I delivered to his face, right, left, right. By the time he hit the ground, I already had my piece in my hand. They heard me cock it. My voice was real cold with anger when I asked them, "Is he worth dying for?" They didn't move. "I didn't think so. Now, pull your pants down and lie on your bellies with your hands behind your heads." They hesitated. I shrugged. "Alternatively I blow your kneecaps off. You choose."

They chose to pull down their pants and lie on their bellies with their white asses in the air.

I put Dehan in the car, slammed the door, and climbed in the other side. They were still lying there as I pulled out onto Left-hand Canyon Drive and headed back toward Seven Hills.

THIRTEEN

FOR A WHILE, THE ONLY SOUND WAS THE GROWL OF THE engine. I kept my eyes on the rearview mirror, waiting for the headlamps to appear, trying to think what I would do if they came after us. But all there was was blackness, and ahead, the hazy funnels of light, casting the blacktop into sharp relief, and making demons out of the tall pines that loomed over the road.

Pretty soon, we came to Lickskillet Road. I slowed, killed the lights, and crawled onto the dirt track, climbing slowly, bumping and grinding, until we came to the crossroads at Gold Hill. There I turned left and headed for Seven Hills at a steady twenty miles per hour. After five minutes, I put my headlamps on again and accelerated.

I glanced at Dehan. She had an idiot smile on her face that made me laugh. She said, "That was so cool."

"What was?"

"You were, like, a hero, defending my honor. Nobody has ever done that for me, Stone." She giggled. "You are my hero." She giggled again.

"Glad to hear it, kiddo."

She turned her dopey smile on me. "Am I your princess?"

"Sure. You know it."

"Like a fairy tale."

"Yup."

She heaved a huge sigh. "All I ever wanted." I didn't answer and we drove in silence. "Does that sound weird to you?"

"What?"

"All I ever wanted." Before I could answer she said it again, exaggerating all the vowel sounds. "Aall Aye Ehvah Oo-On-tEd. Aall Aye Ehvah Oo-On-tEd. It's so weird."

She started giggling again. Soon, the giggles became helpless laughter, which eventually subsided into a blissful sigh. "Aall Aye Ehvah Oo-On-tEd . . . Have I let you down?"

"Not at all."

"Coz that's the last thing Aye Ehvah Oo-On-tEd."

She subsided into helpless laughter again.

Ahead, the soft glow of Seven Hills appeared over the wooded slopes. I said quietly, "We're almost there."

She returned to her dopey smile. "Hmmm . . . that sounds nice. Almost there. There. There is that place where we all want to be. And that is where my hero is taking me. There. Almost *there*."

I pulled into the lot and helped her out of the car. She embraced my right arm and rested her head on my shoulder as we climbed the steps to the reception. It dawned on me that Ned had not given us a second room yet. We had been out all day and he had obviously forgotten in the evening. There was no one on reception when we entered and, looking at the state she was in, it struck me it might be wise not to leave her alone.

We got to the room and I sat her on the bed to take her boots off, then helped her to the bathroom to brush her teeth. She was unsteady on her feet.

"How many puffs did you take, Dehan?"

"Three."

"Is that all? How come you're so stoned?"

She giggled. "Stoned. That's your name. Three for every one that everybody else took."

She made her way unsteadily back to the bed while I brushed my teeth. I could hear her voice through the open door.

"We're friends, Stone. More than friends. Pals, buddies, compadres, partners . . . You're my hero. I'm your princess . . ."

I was chuckling to myself, thinking how embarrassed she was going to be in the morning. I stepped out of the bathroom and froze. She had her blouse off and was pulling off her jeans. She grinned at me and waved a finger in a negative gesture. "Oh no, mister. I am leaving my bra and panties *on*. No funny stuff, Mister Hero."

She rolled back onto the bed and slipped under the covers. To my relief, she seemed to go straight off to sleep. I took off my shoes but left the rest of my clothes on and got in under the covers. I switched off the light and closed my eyes.

That was when she flung her arm around me, snuggled up, and murmured, "Aall Aye Ehvah Oo-On-tEd." And began softly to snore.

DEHAN SLEPT LIKE A LOG. I slept little and fitfully. At six, I slipped out from under her arm and went into the bathroom to shower. I shaved gratefully and restored order to my hair, then dressed in my usual clothes. I checked my messages on my laptop, but there was nothing yet regarding Kathleen's credit card, phone, and email records.

At seven I went down and ordered bacon, eggs, and a gallon of coffee. I didn't expect Dehan before nine, possibly later, but she appeared at half past seven and ordered the same as me, with extra toast and a jug of fresh orange juice. She sat at the table without saying anything and finally looked at me. I couldn't help smiling.

"Good morning, princess."

"Stone, I am so sorry. I don't know what to say."

"Don't sweat it."

The waitress came with her orange juice and coffee and

refilled my cup while she was there. When she'd gone, Dehan asked, "Stone, did we . . . ?"

"What?"

"I was . . . I was undressed. Did we . . . ?"

"Oh!" I laughed. "No! No, of course not." I shook my head for good measure. "Not at all."

"Oh." She nodded. "Okay. Good." Then she frowned. "Not that that would be awful! I mean . . . It wouldn't be right, but . . ."

"Dehan."

"What?"

"It's cool. We're cool. We're good. Eat, drink. We need to review what we learned last night, and where it leaves us."

"Where it leaves us . . . ?"

I laughed. "I mean about the case. I need you focused."

She nodded. "Yes."

She drained a glass of orange juice and refilled it, pulled off half of that, and I started talking.

"Okay, let's look at what we know so far. We know that on Friday, sixth July, at three forty in the afternoon, Kathleen left New York by train. It takes about forty hours, by train and bus, to get from New York to Boulder."

I sipped my coffee while Peaches and Cream delivered Dehan's breakfast. I was accustomed to seeing the intense concentration with which Dehan attacked good food. But this morning was kind of special. I gave her a moment, till I saw the color returning to her cheeks. Eventually, she glanced at me and I carried on.

"Now, we don't actually know where, when, or even *if* Kathleen arrived in Colorado—*alive*. All we know is that having boarded her train in New York, she turned up dead in Lefthand Canyon."

She nodded her agreement, dunked toast into a fried egg, and stuffed it in her mouth. Then she spoke with difficulty.

"Bud we mush ashoom she awibed at reesht in Jenba."

"We must assume she arrived at least in Denver. Agreed. And

that would have happened at about eight a.m. on Sunday. Now, either she rented a car or she was picked up."

Dehan nodded. "Mhm."

"We'll be able to confirm from her emails whether she rented a car, but I am pretty sure she didn't. No abandoned cars were found at or near the scene. Either way, I am going to trouble my dear Watson to check if any rented cars were reported stolen at that time. For now at least, let's proceed on the assumption that she did not rent a car.

"That means either Ingrid and/or Alfredo picked her up, Greg picked her up, or Sly or one of his men picked her up. Which brings us to last night."

I paused. She was stacking bacon and fried egg onto a piece of toast. She skewered it all with her fork and maneuvered it into her mouth. She chewed, watching me. "Kib gobbing," she said, with difficulty.

"Keep going?" She nodded. I kept going. "Okay, Greg. Greg is prosperous. From his own admission, we know that he was sweet on Kath at one time, and we know that he resented her getting hitched with Mo. We also know that he was unwilling to be helpful in our investigation and claimed that we were wasting his time. We know, again from his own admission, that he has visited the Shack in the company of Pat, Kathleen's sister. This last confirmed by Saul."

Dehan mopped the last of the egg from her plate with a piece of bread, stuffed it in her mouth, and sat back in her chair with a comfortable smile on her chewing face. She sipped coffee and sighed.

"Everything keeps coming back to two points, Greg and the Shack."

I nodded. "And Kathleen was not involved with either of them. But hold your horses. Let's not start analyzing yet, Little Grasshopper. There are more facts. We know, for example, that Pat took the left-hand path and got involved in drugs, and we can safely infer that the Shack and its patrons played a part in that process."

"Its patrons in the form of the man Sly and El Coyote."

"Precisely so. Now, here is where it gets a bit tricky, because a lot was implied last night, but very little was actually said. Saul said *he thought* Pat had some kind of arrangement with Sly to sell dope in New York. But Sly never actually confirmed that. Equally, Sly said he had *access* to large quantities of cannabis, but he never said he grew it himself. I think it's safe to assume that he does grow some, but we don't know for a fact that he does, how much, or where."

Her eyes and her mouth made three large Os as realization began to dawn. "Oh, mamma. I see where you are going."

"Maybe. It's something we should look into."

"You think Greg is growing cannabis for Sly."

"Think is too strong a word. It's a hunch. Greg has a lot of money and a lot of land. He was sweet on Kath but he was hanging out with Pat. He was a clean-living, clean-cut cowboy hanging out with a dopehead in a joint like the Shack. What would make him do that?"

"Son of a gun."

"Pat's known him most of her life. What happens? She's the black sheep of this Irish-Italian Catholic family. Maybe she decides to make a bit of money and get her independence. So she talks to Greg about growing dope on his land. She talks to Sly about selling it in New York."

Dehan was nodding as I spoke. "Starts out in her mind as a small-scale deal between friends, but it gets out of hand. Before she knows it they're dealing in tens of thousands of dollars. She's in the Big Apple, with too much money and an addictive personality. Next thing, she's spending all her money—and Sly's—on blow and anything else she can get her hands on."

I sighed. "From there, it plays out like we thought. He threatens to send some boys out east to collect his money, and she begs Kathleen to come and either bail her out or plead for time.

We saw last night how that might have worked for her. A pretty, vulnerable woman in the hands of Sly and his Angel friends is not a nice thought."

"Jesus . . ."

"So while we wait for the records, I suggest we talk to the sheriff and ask for the semen sample to be sent to Frank to be tested again. We also get him to check on car rental thefts at the time of the murder, and then we drop in on Public Records and see exactly how far Greg's ranch stretches, and where Sly and Coy live."

FOURTEEN

Dehan rested her ass on the hood of my car and gazed up at the vast, cold, blue Colorado sky, while I phoned the sheriff of Lee County.

"Good morning, Detective Stone. I see you're up nice and early. I wasn't expecting to hear from you so soon, I confess."

"I know that, Sheriff. I am trying to save you trouble and bother. Here's the situation. The way it is, we might be looking at a major drug trafficking syndicate operating out of Gold Hill." I heard a squeak down the line that might have been a "*What?*" but ignored it and plowed right on. "Now, because the operation would involve the sale of drugs in a state other than Colorado, we might be looking at pulling in the FBI, and believe me, once those boys start turning over your laundry, nobody's Y-fronts go unscrutinized, if you take my meaning. And influential people tend to remember that kind of inconvenience when the elections come around."

"Holy . . . !"

"Now, here's the thing. Maybe we can avoid all the bother of a federal investigation, and quietly close down the operation, while solving a murder at the same time and keeping everybody happy, and share out the kudos, if you catch my drift . . ."

I heard him swallow. "Any way I can help . . ."

"That's what I hoped you'd say. Cars rented from car hire firms in Denver and Boulder between Friday the sixth of July and Monday the ninth, 2012, *that were reported stolen.* So: stolen car rentals for those dates, from Boulder and Denver."

"Got it."

"Also, I need to know the exact extent and limits of Greg Carson's ranch, and any other land he might own in this district."

"That's easy. You'll find that right there in the library at Seven Hills. Tell Polly I sent you and to give you anything you need."

"Also . . ."

"More?"

"More. Where do Sly and El Coyote live? And do they own or rent any land?"

". . . And all this will prevent the Feds coming up here?"

"Yup."

"Well, I'll get my boy lookin' into the stolen vee-hicles right away. You can find Greg's ranch where I told you, and Sly and Coy, they're a bit weird, but they ain't bad folk. They got a house just at the back of a club called the Shack. How can I explain . . . ?"

"We know where the Shack is."

"You do? You don't waste time, do you? Well if you turn left just after the Shack and follow the track for a mile and a half, that'll bring you to their house."

I thought about it for a moment. "And that same road will bring me to Gold Hill."

"You got it. That's right."

"And I'm going to hazard a wild guess here, Sheriff, but is their house right on the edge of Greg Carson's land?"

"Well, now you mention it, it's *on* Greg's land. Why?"

"Just a hunch."

"Now look here, Stone, I hope you ain't thinking that Greg and Sly and Coy is involved in drug trafficking! They're stand-up, law-abiding folk. I run a peaceful county and I don't want you upsetting people . . ."

"Thanks, Sheriff. You've been very helpful. We'll be in touch."

SEVEN HILLS LIBRARY WAS A SMALL, modern building that tried to emulate Frank Lloyd Wright without taking any of the risks. There was a squat, three-story central tower in white, with two lateral wings made of local stone. The ceilings were high, and there were lots of wooden staircases leading to mezzanine floors. The windows were vast and panoramic, and there was an organically shaped lake at the side of the building with a selection of local trees. However, unlike Lloyd Wright, this architect had kept the forestry on the outside of the building.

The librarian, a woman in her thirties whose smile declared she was determined not to regret wasting her teens and twenties in demure propriety, looked both pleased and surprised to see somebody in her library. She was delighted to lead us to the maps and show us the exact extent of Greg's ranch. It was a full one thousand three hundred hectares of land. It stretched four miles east to west from Gold Hill to well beyond Sly and Coy's house, where Lefthand Canyon Drive turned north. In the south, it was bordered by Fourmile Canyon Drive, giving it a mile's depth in the west and two miles in the east.

"Three generations of Carsons built up that ranch." She said it with all the vicarious pride of one who longed to be a Carson. "Good folk," she added, for good measure, in case we'd missed it.

I offered her the smile of an impressed tourist. "And is there likely to be a fourth generation of Carsons, Polly?"

She simpered. "Well, so far he ain't married, and there doesn't seem to be anybody on the horizon."

I winked. "Maybe he's waiting for a pretty librarian."

She went scarlet with pleasure and hurried back to her desk. We looked at the map. Sly and Coy's house was clearly marked as part of the Carson property, with a good mile of wilderness to the back and to the west, and three miles of mixed pasture land and pine woods to the east. A little over a mile to the north was the Shack.

"Let's see if we can rent a truck somewhere, take a trip down to Fourmile Canyon Drive, and walk up. Two gets you twenty we're going to find a plantation within walking distance of Sly's place, plus a drying and storage shed."

Polly told us that Larry at the gas station had a couple of trucks he lent out to tourists during the season. We thanked her, stepped out into the chilly, sunlit, organic garden, and took a stroll down Main Street to the gas station. There we bought a local map and rented a Dodge truck from Larry. Larry was wearing blue dungarees and a blue cap, and managed to make words in spite of the odd mismatch between his remaining teeth and his mouth. He grinned a lot and seemed to be buoyed by some secret source of happiness.

"Yiz can go dahn t'Gold Heel 'n theen come all t'way beck t'Salina, but tha's n'awful long way t'go, when all y'godda do is, take a lift at Emanciation Hill n'cut cross country dahn t'Salinas. 'S half the time and gits y'there all'same. S'what I'd do. Fourmile Creek Drive starts right there, in Salina."

We thanked him warmly and, once we'd worked out what he'd said, took his advice.

It ended up being a ten-and-a-half-mile drive in two big loops, through deep canyon gorges in some of the most remote and beautiful terrain I had ever seen. We made Salina after about five miles, which took all of half an hour, and then crawled south and eventually west along Fourmile Canyon Drive. That was another six miles, until my GPS told me we had come parallel with Sly and Coy's house, a mile north of our location.

We were in a broad, grassy esplanade with steep, densely forested slopes on either side. I pulled off the track, we grabbed a rucksack we'd packed with sandwiches and water, and we began our climb through the woods. It was a cold day, the sun was in the south, and the trees were dense, but even so, after five minutes of climbing, scrabbling on the loose pine needles, and hauling ourselves up manually through the trees, where the slopes were steepest, we were hot and perspiring.

After about fifteen minutes, the slope leveled off a bit and the trees thinned out. Dehan leaned her back against a large pine, checked the GPS on her phone, and pointed up to our left.

"Another climb, old-timer, it's up there."

"Old-timer?" I followed her across a gully, crunching over dry twigs and branches, toward the second slope. "You didn't call me that last night, when I defended your honor."

"Shut up."

We scrambled, clawed, and climbed for another fifteen minutes, and finally the ground leveled off again and we found ourselves at the edge of the forest looking out at a huge clearing, maybe three hundred and fifty yards south to north, and double that across, east to west. We dropped on our bellies to have a look, and get a rest.

Opposite us, there was another stretch of woodland, and I knew that beyond that, maybe half a mile away, was Sly's house. But over on the left, hidden from the road by that forest, was exactly what we had come looking for. A long, broad area of land which had been recently disturbed, as though it had been harvested. At a rough estimate, I guessed it was at least sixty yards across and a good hundred and fifty yards long. You need a patch six feet across to grow an outdoor cannabis plant successfully, and in the right conditions it will grow to well over seven feet and give you three to five pounds of produce. The plot we were looking at here, at a rough estimate, would support about five hundred plants.

Dehan jerked her head toward the field. "If he's planting super skunk there . . ." She sucked her teeth and thought for a moment. "From a patch like that, he's harvesting maybe seven hundred and fifty kilos, maybe a ton of weed a year. Wholesale value, say two, two and a half grand a kilo, you're looking at maybe two million bucks."

I nodded. "Tax free. No wonder he looks prosperous. But he might be growing corn. We need to get a closer look."

We went at a steady jog, keeping to the tree cover, and circled around until we were within ten feet of the edge of the field. There we dropped and lay among the ferns, listening. There was only the sigh of the pines and the odd flap of wings. After about five minutes, when we were sure there was nobody about, we moved forward to the churned-up earth and squatted down to inspect it.

Everywhere we looked, there were the severed stems of the cannabis plants. They had been harvested whole and taken away to a barn somewhere, there to have the buds removed and prepared for wholesale. I took out my cell and photographed the area, and the severed stems. Dehan sighed and shoved her hands in her back pockets.

"Okay, so we've proved, for our own satisfaction, that Greg is growing marijuana on his ranch. We've proved that Sly lives on that ranch in rented accommodation, two or three hundred yards from the plantation." She shook her head at me. "But none of that is illegal. So far, there is no crime here."

"I know. We have also proved that Sly sold dope to Pat, and she probably sold it on in New York, but that's all circumstantial. We still haven't connected any of this to Kathleen or her murder." I spread my hands. "We're making progress. We are putting together the pieces. What we need to do now is prove that Sly is selling this stuff illegally, and connect him, through Pat, to Kathleen."

She chewed her lip. "How are we going to do that?"

I pointed at the woods that separated us from Sly. "Let's take a look at his house, see if the drying shed is there. If it is, right now there should be a ton of weed drying inside it."

She snorted and we moved in among the trees. "A ton of weed. I'd hate to think what would happen to Happy Valley if that barn caught fire."

"You're a bad woman, Dehan."

A few minutes later, we were lying among the ferns again. Ahead of us was a large, two-story clapboard house, about fifty yards away. Out front there was a Buick, and beside it a Range Rover. Beyond it, we could see the road that led east to Gold Hill and west down to the Shack, but much closer, about fifteen or twenty yards away, up against the trees, there was a large barn with a heavy padlock on the door. And the smell emanating from it was unmistakable.

I smiled at her. "Bingo."

She raised an eyebrow. "Yeah, bingo, but now what?"

"We wait till dark, then we go in and photograph the stuff."

"And then?"

I lay with my chin on my arms, chewing my lip. And then? And then what? I looked at her and we stared at each other for a bit in silence. Eventually, she said, "We can't stake them out and wait for a buyer to show up, to see where he's from and where he goes. We haven't got the time or the resources. And neither has the sheriff."

"I know."

"Even if Sly and Coy and Greg are in partnership to grow and sell weed, it's still legal. We need that connection to Pat and Kathleen."

"I know, I know . . ." I sighed. "Let's see what we discover inside. Maybe we'll find something so we can force their hands somehow . . ."

And we lay there, eating sandwiches and watching the house and the barn as the sun slid down in the west.

FIFTEEN

Eventually, late afternoon, with its russet light and its elongated shadows, faded into a grainy dusk. The sun died on the western peaks and there spilled its blood over the Rocky Mountains. The light went out of the sky, and the vast translucent mantle was pierced, one by one, by icy stars. In the house, windows began to glow, while not so far off, the coyotes began to howl. And just above our heads, an owl told us that what we were about to do was a really bad idea.

But what would he know? He was just an owl.

I looked at Dehan. "Let's go."

We crouch-ran the short distance to the barn. She touched my shoulder and pointed to the corner of the building. "I've got this. Keep watch."

I raised an eyebrow at her, but for once in my life I did as I was told. It didn't take long. Fifteen seconds later, the padlock was off and we were easing the rickety door open on its rollers. The smell was overpowering, like boiling cabbage on steroids. We slipped through the gap and pulled the door closed behind us. It was very dark. I felt Dehan's breath on my ear.

"Did you see any windows?"

"No, but I couldn't see the east wall."

"You've got a flashlight on your key ring."

"I know. I put it there."

"Use it!"

"Give me a chance, will you."

I pulled it from my pocket and switched it on, shielding it with my hand and directing it down toward the floor. By its dim glow, we examined the wall on the right. It was enough to see that there were no windows, so I played the thin beam around the barn. There were long stretches of nylon cord suspended from wall to wall, at a height of about seven feet, some four or five feet apart. I didn't count them, but there must have been eight or ten at least. I nudged Dehan and pointed at them.

"For drying. He must have another barn somewhere. That wouldn't take five hundred plants."

She nodded. "He must have harvested in mid-September. He's already dried the plants and processed them. That's fast work."

"With a bit of luck, he has it stored here. Let's have a look."

The whole area was about thirty by sixty feet, with a high ceiling and a loft. From where I was standing, the loft seemed to be empty. We found the dope among the shadows at the back. Most of it was in big plastic drums, maybe thirty gallons in volume. But there was a large stack of smaller, five-gallon tubs, weighing about eight or ten pounds. It was hard to tell. Then, over in the right-hand corner, we found a huge stash, eight feet high, of plastic packages sealed with packing tape. Each one about two pounds—a kilo.

There were rolls of tape and plastic bags in a carton nearby.

I turned to Dehan. "I'm willing to bet that the labs researching the medical benefits of cannabis have slightly stricter shipping requirements."

"You think?"

We took photographs and video footage, both of which would be inadmissible as evidence in a court of law, and in any case proved only that Greg was cultivating and storing cannabis, which in Colorado was perfectly lawful. It would, however, be something to show the captain, and possibly the sheriff.

"If we get a result from Kathleen's credit card records, or her phone and email, this may give us enough to pull the three of them in for questioning, and Pat too. Then we can try to prove a link."

She sighed. "Yeah, Pat's going to be key to this, if we're right. She's the bridge. But so far we haven't got much, Sensei. Let's go, this place gives me the creeps."

We headed back toward the big doors, following the small, hazy circle from my flashlight. I was thinking of the long, difficult trek back through the woods to the Dodge and wondering if, when we got to the Wagon Wheel, there would be any news from the 43rd. Despite Dehan's downbeat assessment, I had a feeling we were approaching a turning point in the case.

I wasn't wrong.

There was a loud, shuddering noise of wood and rollers, and a translucent oblong of starlight opened up ahead of us. Four black silhouettes stood stenciled against it. We froze, but the glare from two powerful lamps blinded us and bathed us in white light. I shaded my eyes, and the glare and the silhouettes seemed to warp and swell as I heard the trudge of boots on the dirt floor.

A nicotine-stained voice rasped, "*Denle a la luz!*"

A moment later there was a buzzing and flickering overhead and four neon tubes bathed the barn in a dead, humming glow. El Coyote was staring at us. He was flanked by two Angels. One of them I recognized as Scott, the ape I'd decked the night before. He was grinning among his bruises. A fourth guy who looked Mexican was returning from the switch panel by the door.

Coy eyed us with what you could only describe as loathing. "You fockin' lying shit. I'm gonna gut you like a fish, Gringo. But first we gonna play a bit with your *puta*."

Scott looked happy and laughed. Dehan disturbed me by laughing too. "You wanna go first, Coy? I'm gonna bust your balls so hard they'll knock your eyes out of their sockets, *pendejo*! And you?" She pointed at Scott. "You're gonna be singing soprano in the Colorado State Opera."

El Coyote looked more like an iguana than a wild dog. He was motionless and expressionless, and his voice came out like a quiet hiss in his throat. "You got a big mouth, *puta*. But we gonna silence it for you."

I caught Dehan's eye and nodded once. I pulled my piece and aimed it at Coy's forehead, right between his eyes. Dehan had her .38 in her hands and was covering the other three by turns.

I said, "This is how it's going to go down. Coy, you are going to lie on your face. Scott, you are going to tie his hands and his ankles. You two"—I gestured at the other Angel and the Mexican—"you're going to do the same. Understood? Then, Scott, you're going to tie up your Mexican pal over there. Nobody gets hurt. Okay?"

El Coyote snarled and managed for a moment to look like a wild dog. "Nobody fockin' move. These mothers are cops. I can *smell* it. They on private property and they ain't gonna shoot nobody."

Dehan grinned. "See, *pendejo*, you're right, and then again, you're wrong. Yeah, we are cops, but look around, pal. Where are your credible witnesses? Blink in a way I don't like and I'll nail you. And if there's anybody left to get on a witness stand, who do you think the jury is going to believe?"

It was a brave attempt, but it didn't work. Coy snarled something obscene in Spanish, then shouted, "*Kill them!*" and charged me, closely followed by his three gorillas.

I screamed, "*Run!*" at Dehan and fired. But Coy was already past my gun and had gripped me in a crushing embrace, hurling me to the ground. I landed with a *whoosh!* and felt blades of pain pierce my winded lungs. Over his shoulder I saw, as though in slow motion, Dehan's gun kick. The empty shell spiraled into the air, and the Mexican looked astonished and sat down, staring at the oozing hole in his chest.

The two Angels were charging her. I screamed again, "*Run!*

Run!" She dodged Scott's lunge and drove her elbow into his floating ribs. He staggered back and dropped to his knees. I tried to line up the other guy, but they were moving fast, and the risk of hitting Dehan was too great.

Then Coy was straddling me, with his knees on my arms, pulling back his fist to smash me in the face. I pressed the muzzle of my automatic against his thigh and pulled the trigger. There was a muffled *phut!* and El Coyote was howling like his namesake. I threw him on the ground and scrambled to my feet. The second Angel had Dehan pinned against the wall, trying to hook her legs from under her with his heel. I was about to charge him, but stopped and frowned. I saw her slip her .38 into her waistband and bend her knees. Next thing, her right hand slammed up and gripped his balls. He choked and she called out to me, "This what they call Colorado oysters, Stone?" Then she squeezed hard and twisted. The noise that came out of that man's mouth was not human.

He fell. She kicked Scott in the head and said, "*Now* we can run."

We ran.

Dehan is young and athletic. I am neither, plus I was badly winded from El Coyote's tackle. As I came through the barn doors, she was already moving in among the trees and disappearing. I stumbled and stopped a moment to get my breath, and that was when I felt the muzzle against my head and heard the click of a hammer.

"Don't move." I froze. "Okay, now give me your gun, and put your hands behind your head."

For the second time that night, I did as I was told. I felt a strong grip on my right wrist, and next thing, my arms were wrenched behind my back, a plastic zip tie bit into my skin, and my hands were bound behind my back.

I said, "I'm a cop. You're making a bad mistake."

"I know who you are, pal. Turn around." I turned and found myself looking into Greg Carson's smug face. "You may be a cop,

Stone, but you're out of your jurisdiction and breaking the law on my property. I am in my perfect right to shoot you dead, and I may just do that."

I gave my head a twitch. "Well, Greg, I don't know what to tell you. If you are convicted for the murder of Kathleen Olvera, that will be in New York. You'll get life. But if you are convicted of kidnapping and killing a police officer, in the performance of his duty, that'll be here in Colorado, and you know as well as I do that the DA will be looking for the death penalty. Now it's up to you to make a smart choice, knowing that right now my partner is on her way back to New York with information about what we just found in your barn."

He smiled and shook his head. "Sorry, pal, it was dark, you did not identify yourself, and you shot and murdered one of my tenants. You don't stand a chance."

He raised his gun and pointed it at my head. "Get back in there. I want to talk to you before I kill you."

"How can I refuse?"

I went back into the barn where El Coyote was sitting, tying one of his bootlaces around his thigh. He was shaking and looked real pale. Scott was still unconscious, and the other Angel was curled in the fetal position, whimpering. The thought crossed my mind that she had probably castrated him. Greg looked at the scene of carnage and shook his head. He laughed, and I like to think there was a touch of admiration in his voice.

"Boy, you two are somethin', huh? These *hombres* think they're hard, but you just whipped their asses."

"Let's cut to the chase, Greg, and get real. We are police officers. We're here at the invitation of the local sheriff, conducting a murder investigation. So far you haven't broken the law. The best thing you can do is cooperate before this gets any more out of hand."

He put his revolver into his waistband behind his back, studied my face for a moment, and nodded. Then he smashed his fist into my jaw and the lights went out.

SIXTEEN

WHEN I CAME AROUND, THE WORLD WAS A DEEPLY unsatisfactory place. Everything hurt. Within the generalized pain that was existence right then, there were sharper, meaner pains. There was the pain in my back that was making it hard to breathe. There was the pain that was biting into my wrists, the pain that was making my legs shake, and, above all, the blunt axe that somebody had left wedged into my skull. There were other pains too, but they were just the background.

It slowly filtered into my mind that I was tied to one of the wooden pillars that held up the roof of the barn. Putting my weight on my feet eased the pain in my back and shoulders, and I was able to peer around me. Gradually, they came into focus. They'd brought chairs and they were sitting, watching me.

There was Greg, up close, with no particular expression on his face. A bit farther back was El Coyote. He looked feverish and pasty. He was sweating, and another Mexican-looking guy was dressing the wound in his leg. The Angel was over on the right, not far from where he'd fallen. He was still in the fetal position, but he'd gone quiet. He looked like he might be unconscious. Scott was lying next to him. The body of the guy she'd shot had disappeared, but there were two more live ones in his place, standing, looking at me with hatred in their eyes. Sitting in front of them, next to Greg, was Sly. It was not a promising scene to wake up to.

Greg reached down by his feet and picked up what at first looked like a coil of rope.

"You know what this is, Stone? This is a bullwhip. It will take the skin clean off a man's back. I can kill a man with this whip. I know that 'cause I've done it. An' believe me, it is not a nice way to go. You don't wanna go that way if you can avoid it. This here will make a strong man weep like a baby and beg for his mommy."

I sighed. "Have you any idea, Greg, how much trouble you're in?"

Sly leaned back and shrieked with laughter. Greg just smiled and shook his head. "I gotta say, Stone. I don't respect many men, but I have a grudging respect for you." He turned to look at Sly, who was still braying like a donkey, and started to laugh. "Can you believe the balls on this guy? He's tied to a post, hand and foot, he's on his own, unarmed in the middle of the Rocky Mountains, surrounded by a gang of desperados who hate his guts. And he goes right ahead and says, 'Do you know how much trouble you're in?'"

Sly became helpless, Greg's shoulders were shaking, and the Angels had started to laugh too. He had a point. But I wasn't going to tell him that.

"Do you know how long it's going to be before the Feds are crawling all over you like flies on shit, Greg?"

He was still chuckling. "Why don't you tell me?"

"What you have tied up here, Greg, is a man, John Stone. You have *not* got federal law enforcement tied up here. What is this, some anti–world government militia shit? You think because you're in the wilderness you can buck the federal system? Believe me, Greg, they don't like it when redneck anarchists start killing law enforcement agents. It upsets them a lot."

"We ain't gonna kill nobody, city boy. I have no idea who is gonna kill you. I guess you're gonna go out there and upset one of them wild old mountain boys, and he's gonna shoot you dead. And good old Sheriff Watson, and my uncle the judge, will explain that good ol' Greg Carson is a pillar of the community, and he would never hurt nobody, least of all an officer of the law. Let's face it, Stone, you're screwed."

I was beginning to think he was right, and wondering how far Dehan had got and whether she had contacted the FBI.

"So why haven't you killed me already?"

He nodded, assessing me with his eyes. "Because Sly and Coy and me was all wondering what the hell you're doing here."

"I told you. We're investigating the murder of Kathleen Olvera."

He was already shaking his head before I'd finished. "Uh-uh, you ain't selling me that horseshit. Why'd you break and enter into my barn? What were you doing at the Shack trying to buy dope?"

I narrowed my eyes at him. "You advised us to go there, remember?"

He looked at me like I was crazy. "I told you Pat had friends in the off-grid crowd. I didn't tell you to go there an' pose as fuckin' drug dealers. You really upset the boys, you know? That was some special kind of stupid what you done there, Stone."

Coy spoke. His voice was weak. "You should have told us he was coming . . ."

Greg's face twisted with contempt. He half turned. "Hey, Sancho Panza, when I come down to Rancho Puta in Mexico, you can tell me what to do. But while you're here, you keep your mouth shut. *Comprende?*"

"*Pendejo . . .*"

"Open your mouth again, Coy, an' I'm gonna tear that leg off and shove it up your ass. Now have we concluded this conversation, or do you need me to demonstrate?"

Sly was wheezing his serpentine laugh. "Boys, let's keep it friendly here, shall we? You tellin' me, Stone, that you went through all them theatrics last night just to investigate that girl's death?"

"That's what I do. It's my job. So satisfy my curiosity. Why did you kill Kathleen?"

"Who says we did?"

"Come on, Sly! What happened? You had this operation going on. Pat was going to take care of sales and distribution for you in the Bronx, but she blew the profits on coke and smack. You got mad, said if she didn't come up with your money, you'd send a couple of your gorillas down to take care of her. So she sent her sweet little sister up to beg for more time. Like you said, Sly, you love Catholic girls."

Greg got to his feet, his whip in hand. "That's some imagination you got there, boy. You gonna have us on death row before you're done."

"You telling me it's not true?"

"I ain't tellin' you jack shit."

I looked over at the Angels, who were leaning against the wall, watching. "What about you boys? You ready for the lethal injection? You know, even if you don't do the killing yourselves, this is joint enterprise. You still go down for it. You ready to do that?"

They glanced at each other but didn't say anything. I pressed on.

"Who was it? Was it you, Coyote? You look to me like a man who could get a kick out of killing a helpless girl. Was it you? Or did you all take a part? You know we're having the semen tested again. Whose is it? Which one of you raped her? Was it you, Sly? You know, that, plus killing a cop, guarantees your injection . . ."

The lash of that whip was the most painful thing I had ever experienced in my life. It burned, but not like fire. It was deeper and more agonizing than fire. It tore into my skin and penetrated deep into my muscles. I swore to myself I would not cry out, but though I clenched my teeth till I thought they'd crack, I couldn't suppress the noise of the sheer agony in my throat.

"I told you it hurts, boy. And I'm warning you, you're really startin' to get me mad. I can't believe you. You're tied to that pole interrogating us! You're something! Now you better start talking, 'cause if you don't, I'm gonna start whipping till you beg me to put you out of your misery, like a stray dog."

"What the hell do you want to know? I've told you why I'm here."

With the second lash I didn't even try. I cried out with every fiber in my body. Maybe self-pity and pleading would come later, but right then all I could feel was an agony of uncontrollable rage.

Sly was giggling, Coy was smiling, and Greg looked smug. I eyed the Angels. They looked skeptical.

Greg said, "I don't believe you, and neither do my associates. I might, just, buy that that lazy slob Sheriff Watson would ask you to look at his cold case. I might just believe that. But that you would try and buy ten kilos of weed as part of your investigation? No sir, I don't buy that."

"Then what the hell do you think I'm doing here?"

It was Sly who answered. "If you're investigating Kathleen's murder . . ." He spread his hands. "Pat was from the Bronx, I'm guessing Kathleen was too, am I right, Greg?"

"Yeah."

"So *you* are from the Bronx. Like me. We *all* from the Bronx. Now I have to say that the only thing, in my experience, more twisted, sick, and corrupt than a crook from the Bronx is a cop from the Bronx. So I'll tell you why *I* think you're here, Stone. I think you and your bitch are here to steal *my* dope!"

I curled my lip at him. "Use your brain, you stupid asshole! Why would I steal your dope? If I could sell it in the Bronx I'd need everything you have in this damn store plus twice as much again! You'd be worth a thousand times more to me as a partner than stealing from you!"

Coyote spoke again. "It don't make sense. None of it make sense. And I don't like it because it don't make sense. Kill the son of a bitch and finish! Cut off his fockin' head and bury him in the forest."

I smiled through the pain. "Thank you, Coyote. You just confirmed what I suspected."

Greg asked, "What are you talkin' about?"

"Stop playing dumb, Greg. You know as well as I do that's how Kathleen died. After he raped her, he cut off her head and buried her in the woods."

He turned and stared at Coy. "That true? Did you kill her?"

I laughed. I felt light-headed and trippy with the pain, like I was beginning to hallucinate. "Good try, Greg. But this is joint enterprise, remember? One of you did it, you all did it." I looked over at the Angels, who were frowning. "You getting this, boys? Your allegiance is to your chapter and the club, not to these bozos. You better start thinking about copping a plea."

The lash bit into my chest, and for a moment I thought I was going to pass out. But I told myself I was getting to them, causing a rift, however small. And all the while they were whipping me, Dehan was getting away. I knew that by the time she got help, it would probably be too late for me. But she'd finish the job, she'd nail them, and above all, she'd get away.

I raised my head and looked deep into Greg's eyes. "You're the smart one here, Greg. Rape, murder, and mutilation, followed by the kidnapping, torture, and murder of an investigating police officer. There isn't a man in this barn who isn't eligible for the death sentence." They were all staring at me now, and they were all thinking hard. "I don't know which one of you did it. But I know who I *think* did it." I stared at Sly and then past him at El Coyote. "So my advice to all of you is, if you were not directly involved, you'd better start thinking about how to mitigate. Because my partner got away, and you can bet your sorry asses that right now she is on the phone to the Denver field office of the FBI."

Coyote rasped, "Kill the motherfocker! Bury him in the fockin' forest! They will never find him! We deny everything! What fockin' proof have they got?"

Greg turned on him, bellowing, "*I told you when you came to me I didn't want none of this shit! You told me it would be cool!*"

"It is cool, brother. Chill . . ." It was Sly. "Coyote is right, man. We cut his throat. Dig a grave, let Mother Nature take care of him. We deny everything. They can't prove shit."

Greg threw down his whip and pointed at Coyote. "I ain't a part of this. I ain't even here. If this goes bad, I will testify against each one of you, and I will see you on death row. This is *exactly* what you said would *not* happen!"

I watched him stomp all the way down to the big sliding door. I noticed it was open a few inches. He heaved it open enough to step out and pulled it closed again. I felt sick and light-headed. Sly was grinning. "My friend, Coyote, I think you would like the pleasure, wouldn't you?"

"You bet your *fockin'* ass!"

He staggered to his feet and pulled a long, savage blade from his belt.

SEVENTEEN

HE HOBBLED UP AND LEANED AGAINST ME, SO HIS BELLY and his chest were pushed against mine. He grabbed my hair with his left hand and pressed the blade of his knife against my throat. His breath stank of tobacco, beer, and filth. I could see the pores of his skin and the veins in his yellow eyes.

"You ain't gonna beg for mercy, Gringo?"

If I said I wasn't scared, I'd be lying. If I said I wasn't terrified, I'd still be lying. But I was damned sure that if I was going to die, I'd go without giving that son of a bitch the satisfaction of seeing my fear. I looked him in the eye and whispered, "Fuck you, Coy."

His muscles tensed. I saw his knuckles go white on the hilt of his knife. I held his eye and thought I was hallucinating when I heard the voice, calm, quiet, and probably the most beautiful sound I had ever heard in my life.

"That's the last thing you are ever going to do, Coyote. I'd think real hard before doing it. Because if I see you twitch, I'm going to blow your head right off your shoulders." Dehan. She had come back. "Now drop the knife and step away from my partner. I'm going to count to three, motherfucker, but I might shoot you on two, or one."

He stepped back and dropped the knife. I felt my body shudder and heard my breath shake.

"Get down on your belly and put your hands behind your head. You two!" She jerked her chin at the Angels. "Get the packing tape from the corner over there. Truss him up. Hands behind his back. And his ankles. Don't make this complicated. I am outnumbered, jittery, and *real* pissed, and I don't know what I might do if you rile me."

One of them scurried away to get the packing tape while the other looked from me to Dehan and back again. "We never had nothin' to do with no rape and no murder. We just deliver the weed. We tried to dissuade Scott last night, honest we did." He looked over his shoulder. "Didn't we, Joe?"

"Shut up."

He sighed and looked at Sly, who was rocking back and forth, singing a little song to himself, "Oh boy, oh boy, oh boy . . ."

The Angels bound Coy and then did the same for Sly and Scott, who was beginning to regain consciousness. Then Dehan had one of them bind the other, and she cuffed the last and taped his ankles together. Finally, she cut my bonds and supported me as I gained my feet. I was unsteady, but as determined not to show any weakness in front of her as I had been to hide it from El Coyote, only for different reasons.

She looked anxiously into my face. "You okay?"

"I'm fine. We need to get Greg."

"He's trussed up outside, like a Christmas turkey."

I smiled at her. "You're a piece of work, Dehan. You know that?"

"What?" She said it defiantly, looking around at the gang. They were like a bunch of giant cocoons. "You don't like my work? I say we stage a gang fight and shoot the bastards with their own guns."

The Angels protested loudly that they didn't deserve that and had no idea of what was going down at the ranch. I ignored them.

"The idea has its appeal, Detective, but it may be best if we call the sheriff."

She sighed noisily. "Fine, if you insist. By the way." She held up her phone. "I have the last ten minutes on video. It makes entertaining viewing."

"I bet."

I pulled my own phone from my pocket and dialed the sheriff's number. I checked my watch. It was almost eight.

"Stone, you again. How can I help you *this* time?"

"You can start by canning the sarcasm, Sheriff. I have just been kidnapped and bullwhipped by three of your stand-up, law-abiding constituents. One of them was about to cut my throat. You also have a barn full of marijuana here, which was destined for, amongst other places, New York, where it is illegal. That's for starters, Sheriff. So I suggest you gather up some deputies, along with your nicest manners, and get yourself over to Greg Carson's ranch. You're going to need the ME and a meat wagon too. You have one dead Hells Angel, another with a bad concussion, and a third with badly busted balls. Plus, you have four more trussed up and ready to go into custody. It's going to be a busy night for you. Welcome to law enforcement."

He was making lots of noises, but I wasn't listening to any of them. I hung up and turned to Dehan. "Thank you."

She punched my arm, gently. "It was my turn, big guy."

ABOUT HALF AN HOUR LATER, the sheriff came rolling into the ranch in his truck. Behind him, he had four deputies in two cars, and behind them, there was an ambulance and the medical examiner. The esplanade in front of Greg's house was flooded with red-and-blue pulsing lights and uniformed men spilling from their vehicles with worried looks on their faces. Dehan led them toward the barn, along with the ambulance and the ME, and I walked over to the sheriff.

Before he could open his mouth, I shook my head. "This one

didn't start in the Bronx, Watson. This one is all yours, and you'd better notify the DA's office tomorrow. Greg Carson grows the dope here on his farm, with the help of Sly and Coy. They dry it and package it, then they ship it to states where it is not legal, like New York, so they can sell it at a big profit. He was using Pat Olvera for that purpose, and I am pretty close to proving that that connection was what got Kathleen killed.

"They kidnapped me and attempted to murder both me and my partner. She has it on video, and I'm going to ask your ME to take photographs of these." I gestured to my ripped, bloodstained shirt. "This was done with a bullwhip. The whip is in the barn. You need to bag it and send it to the lab. It has Greg's prints on it, and my DNA."

He was squinting resentfully at me. "You brought all this with you from New York."

I shook my head. "No, Sheriff, it was already here. You just needed some police work to find it. It's what they elected you sheriff for." He curled his lip. I ignored him. "Come. I'll give you a tour of the scene."

He went to follow me, but I put my hand on his chest and came up close to look him in the eye. "Just let me tell you something before we go any further. I want Greg locked up in isolation where he cannot talk to anybody until I get to him. If this investigation is not done by the book, or if these boys get off, I am personally going to have the Feds go over Lee County with a fine-tooth comb, and nothing—and I mean *nothing*—will go unexamined. Am I clear?"

He nodded.

"Right. Now let me show you how to go over a crime scene."

AN HOUR LATER, after the paramedics had dressed my lashes, the sheriff had one of his deputies drive us back to Seven Hills. The return journey was more straightforward, because we didn't have to go via Fourmile Canyon Drive and Salina. He also promised he'd have someone go and collect the Dodge in the morning. By the time we got to the Wagon Wheel, it was almost ten, but Peaches and Cream Sr. volunteered to cook us a meal when she saw the state we were in and heard that I'd been bull-whipped and almost had my throat cut. She said that these constituted exceptional circumstances. I had to agree. While she cooked, we went up and showered and changed our clothes.

While Dehan was in the bathroom, I checked my laptop. There was still no news from the captain.

Downstairs, we ordered a couple of stiff whiskeys and sat in front of the fire, which by now was dying toward embers, and sipped while we waited for our food. I hadn't much appetite, but Dehan insisted, with a kind of intense sincerity, that I needed first-class protein to repair the damage. When I tried to argue, she said, "Remember what my mother said! 'You'll die, but foist you'll eat!'"

I laughed painfully. "I thought that was your grandmother."

"It varies," she said, gazing without humor at the smoldering wood. "It's the collective superego of the female side of my father's family."

"Wow . . . You only say that because you know I'm too weak to defend myself." She snorted and we sat in silence for a bit. Finally, as the whiskey began to take effect, I said, "Thanks, Dehan."

She glanced at me and there were tears in her eyes. "I thought you were right behind me, you fuckin' asshole."

I smiled. "By the time I made it to the door, Greg was waiting for me with a gun. I thought you'd gone to get the Feds."

"No." She frowned. "When I reached the plantation, I realized you weren't there. I thought maybe you'd been . . ." The muscles in her jaw bunched and she looked away. She took a slug, swallowed, and then took a deep breath. "I searched for you in the woods. When I didn't find you, I realized you must still be back at the barn. So I went back."

"That wasn't smart."

"Who gives a shit? You'd have done the same." My face told her she was right and she went on. "When I got there, I saw they had you tied up . . ." She shrugged and looked sheepish. "But they weren't torturing you or anything. Also, you wily bastard, you had them talking. So I thought, as long as they were talking and they weren't hurting you, I'd record what they said."

Our bison steaks arrived, along with a bottle of wine. The first mouthful was hard, but the second was easier, and aided by a couple of glasses of Napa Valley merlot, it soon tasted like the most perfect medicine I'd ever taken.

Sleepy, comfortably numb, and with my joints slowly seizing up, Dehan supported me up to what was still our room. By now I didn't even question it. She closed the door and helped me take off my jacket. I fell carefully on the bed and she pulled off my shoes. Then she helped me under the covers.

"You not going to brush your teeth?"

"Not tonight, Josephine."

She went into the bathroom and prepared for bed. When she came back, she lay down next to me, leaning on her elbow and looking down at my face. She was serious.

"Stone, what happened tonight, when I thought . . ." She hesitated. "When I thought something had happened to you, something bad, I thought I'd . . ."

She was having trouble saying it, and I was exhausted and just inebriated enough to realize that life is too short. So I said, "I know. I've been there, remember?"

We stared at each other for a long moment. We often did when we were thinking, but this was different. I knew I should be worried, but I wasn't. She said, "I know we're partners. But we're friends too, right?"

I smiled. "More like family."

She smiled back. "I got a lot of family. But no one quite like . . ." She paused again, reached out, and placed her hand gently on the raw wound on my chest. "I don't know what I would have done . . ."

The knock at the door made us both jump. She hesitated a moment, then sat up quickly and went to open it. It was Ned.

"I am so sorry to disturb you, Detectives. I'd thought you were still dining. I didn't realize you had come up, and I wouldn't bother you, only I know you were anxious . . ."

"What is it?"

"Well, we finally have another room for you. It's right next door here. I'll leave the key with you and let you sleep. Good night!"

I heard him hurry away and, after a pause, Dehan closed the door. She came and stood at the foot of the bed, holding the key, and smiled down at me.

"You going to be okay on your own?"

I shrugged. It took me a moment to answer. "Of course. I'll be fine. Thanks."

"So I guess I'll go next door, let you sleep in peace."

"You too. No snoring tonight."

She laughed and grabbed her stuff. At the door, she stopped and looked back. "Sleep well, Stone."

I grinned. "It was nice sleeping with you, princess."

"Take a hike. Idiot."

The door closed and I struggled out of bed and into the bathroom, where I had a long, cold shower.

EIGHTEEN

I GOT UP LATE, SHOWERED, DRESSED, AND CHECKED MY email. There was still nothing about Kathleen's records. I went down to the dining room and found Dehan on the phone to the sheriff. She hung up as I sat down, and Peaches and Cream came over to pour me some coffee.

Dehan waved the phone at me. "I called the sheriff. He was very cooperative. We can go over anytime to interrogate the prisoners. How do you want to play it?"

"It would have been nice to have those damned records before we went in. Still, it is what it is." I sighed and thought it through for a minute. "Greg is scared. You saw that. He thought he was onto a safe thing, but it's spiraled out of control. He'll be happy to give us Sly and Coy if he thinks he's going to save his own skin."

She frowned as though she didn't like the idea. "So, offer him a deal?"

I shook my head. "No. I want you to take him first. Let him know I am interrogating Sly and Coy. Make him believe they're spilling their guts and he is going down on a capital charge."

She was nodding. "We can use the Angels too, if we need to. Their story is they thought they were just distributing weed. Now it turns out they're up for murder one. They're panicking and pointing the finger at him and Sly and Coyote."

"Yeah. Make him believe you hate his guts, and your one purpose in life is to bring him down, even if it means letting Coy and Sly walk. I'll do the same with Sly and Coy . . ."

She grinned. "Then we swap. Good cop, bad cop."

"And we don't let Sheriff Watson within a mile of them. Also, we sell him the same line we are selling them."

She frowned. "You think he's bent?"

"No, I think he's lazy and naïve, which in a cop is almost worse. He'd let those SOBs walk just to avoid the paperwork, and tell himself they're good folk at heart, boys will be boys."

"You're not wrong, Sensei. You want breakfast?"

"No, let's get this over with."

JAMESTOWN WAS SMALL AND CUTE, nestled among pine trees on a crossroads between three hills on James Canyon Drive. The sheriff's office, which was attached to the county jail, was between the Town Hall and the Methodist church. It was a wood-paneled, open-plan space with a couple of desks and computers in it. He made a real effort to look pleased to see us when we walked in and even offered us coffee, to which I shook my head.

"I'd like to get started right away and close this case, if that's okay with you. Have you got an interrogation room?"

He smiled and shrugged. "We don't usually have any call for interrogation rooms, but there are a couple or three vacant offices upstairs above the jail you can use."

I stared at him a moment. "These are very dangerous men, Sheriff. I have the scars to prove it. I want deputies watching them every minute. But I do not want Greg or Sly or Coy talking to *anybody* except me and Detective Dehan. If that is not followed to the letter, Sheriff, there will be consequences."

He looked resentful and drew breath to protest. I cut him short. "Consequences, Sheriff. Now, we are going to designate the offices as interrogation rooms one and two. I want Greg in room one; five minutes later I want Sly in room two. I want deputies on the doors, and I'll have that coffee upstairs. Thank you for cooperating, Sheriff."

He scowled at me. "You're welcome, I'm sure. This way."

He showed us up to the second story of the jailhouse. There was a suite of offices up there, and we had the deputies bring Greg up to interrogation room one, where he was cuffed to his chair. I watched Dehan sit opposite him with a look on her face I'd have loved to photograph for posterity. I left them to it.

I put my laptop in a second room, and a couple of minutes later, Sly was led to interrogation room two. Like Greg, he was cuffed to his chair; a deputy handed me a cup of coffee, and we were left alone. I sat for a while in silence, sipping, while he tilted his head this way and that. Finally, I said, "Here is how it's going to play out, Sly. You and Greg and Coy have been separated. The sheriff is cooperating, but I am running this operation. What we have, after last night, is video and audio evidence of the kidnap, torture, and attempted murder of a cop. We have testimony from two police officers of drug trafficking and the attempted kidnapping and murder of those two same cops. You three have ticked all the boxes that the Colorado district attorney needs to apply for the death penalty." I paused to give that time to sink in. "I'd go further, Sly, I'd say it is going to be very hard for the judge *not* to grant the death penalty."

He smiled up at a ceiling he could not see. "You tellin' me this, Detective Stone, because you want to scare me into giving you something."

"Right first time, Sly. But that doesn't mean that what I am saying is not true. You know it is true."

"So quit trying to scare me and tell me what you want."

"I want Kathleen's killer."

"Man, you still on that?"

"And I am going to stay on it until I get what I want. Who killed her, Sly?"

"What makes you think I would even *know* that?"

I sighed. "What do you think Detective Dehan is doing right now?"

"I don't need to think. I know. She's tellin' Greg exactly the same as you are tellin' me. And when she is through tellin' him, she gonna go and tell Coyote. I ain't stupid."

I smiled and labored the irony in the words. "The jury is still out on that one, Sly."

He made a smile that was not amused. "You're funny."

"Yeah, deep down funny, where it's not like funny anymore. Now let's stop playing games. You're on the clock, Sly. If you want a deal, you need to get your bid in before Greg or Coy. First come, first served."

He thought about it. "What kind of deal?"

I heaved another sigh and spread my hands. "Look at it from my point of view, Sly. I know one of you killed her. My question is, which one? And I need to know that simply so that I can offer some closure to her mother and her sister. From my point of view, personally, if you all three go down, I got my man."

"I get it, Stone, you made your point. Stop tryin' to sell me on the deal. Just tell me what the deal is."

"Life, in both senses of the word."

"Some deal . . . I want it in writing from the DA."

"I'll recommend it to the DA. We'll see what he says."

He shook his head and laughed, looking blindly into the air. "Man, you want somethin' for *nothin'*?"

"You're beginning to understand the situation, Sly. *You're* fighting for your life. I'm only fighting to give closure to a family. Who do you think has the edge? Now let's get real. I can go now and phone the DA, tell him that you are prepared to cooperate, but you want a deal, in writing. Now, assuming that he agrees, how long do *you* think it's going to take to draft it and have it sent from Denver?"

"Man . . ."

He was looking distressed. I pushed. "But Sly, you and me

both know that even *that* is unrealistic. Ask yourself, if you were the DA, what would your first question be if I made that call?"

He didn't answer. He just stared into space. So I answered for him.

"He's going to ask me, 'What about the other two?' Let's get even more real, Sly. What do you think is the first thing I am going to do when I have hung up on the DA? I am going to go straight to Greg and say, 'Guess what, Greg, Sly just offered the DA a deal. He sells you down the river in exchange for life. But he wants it in writing. You want to talk to me while we wait for the DA to make up his mind and draft the document?' And then there's Coy . . ."

"*Okay, man!*"

"I'll give you my word, and I will tell the DA that I have given you my word. And right now, Sly, that is the best damned offer you are likely to get."

"*Okay! Okay!*"

"Who killed Kathleen Olvera?"

He did a weird thing, swinging his head from side to side, like he was grooving to music. He spread his hands and made a high-pitched squeaking noise in his throat which eventually turned into, "*Man!* I don't know what you want me to *tell* you!"

I stood, pushing the chair back noisily. "See you at the trial, Sly."

"Wait a minute!"

"Stop wasting my time."

He lifted a hand. "Okay! I told you I am going to cooperate. Just give me a minute."

"Minutes are what you have very few of, Sly. You better start talking or I am walking out of that door and you will not see me again until I testify against you."

"*Boy, you're a hard son of a bitch!*"

"Who killed Kathleen Olvera?"

He spread his hands and appealed to the ceiling. "It was El Coyote, man. But if he don't get the death penalty, he is gonna cut my throat. You *have* to give me protection, you understand?

You tellin' me you gonna spare me the death sentence, but if he don't go down, that *is* a death sentence!"

I sat down again. "I understand. I will make the DA understand that too. Talk."

"It was like you said. Pat was sellin' for us down in the Bronx. But she was broke all the time, you know? She's a dopehead, never got her shit together. She used to hang with Greg and he was always givin' her money." He laughed. "Man, she'd do anythin'— and I do *mean* anythin'—for fifty bucks. So we said to her, she could take the shit, sell it, then give us our cut of the money. That way she could get on her feet. We was helpin' her. Know what I'm sayin'?"

"Yeah, you're regular philanthropists."

He wheezed a laugh. "No, man, I never had no interest in stamps. It worked, for a while, know what I'm sayin'? I can't remember how many times, but it was a few. She took the stuff, sold it, kept her share, and brought us our dough." He creased up his face, like it distressed him. "But she weren't *savin'* it. She was spendin' everythin' she made on shit, coke and meth and bad stuff. It was Greg asked us to help her, 'cause he liked her. But I told him it weren't gonna work. You can't rely on a dopehead like that. It ain't *never* gonna pay off. But he said them girls was like family to him. So we had to help her."

"So what happened?"

"What was always gonna happen, man. She calls and talks to Greg. She sold the shit, five K—it was a lot of cash, man—and she blew it all on coke. I was real mad. Greg says he's gonna make good on the bread and we won't be out'a pocket. But I told him we ain't gonna use her no more. We don't need that kind of problem. He says okay, but Coyote ain't happy." He shook his head again. "Greg, he's a cowboy, me, I'm cool. If I have my money, I'm happy. But Coyote, he's a hard son of a bitch, and where he comes from, man, reputation is everything. He's sayin' this bitch has pissed on his reputation and he has got to cut her."

"Okay, so how do we get from there to Kathleen?"

"Get me a cigarette, man. I'm stressed. I'm shakin', man. You fucked me up."

I stuck my head out the door and got a cigarette from one of the deputies. I lit it and handed it to Sly. His hand was trembling as he smoked.

"It was like you said. Greg must have warned her that Coyote was after her blood, 'cause instead of comin' up to the Shack, she sends her sister to talk to us, plead for mercy, kind'a thing. Know what I'm sayin'?"

"How'd she get to the Shack from Boulder?"

He shrugged. "How should I know? I guess Greg picked her up."

"How did Coy kill her?"

"Don't call him 'Coy,' man. He ain't coy. That really offends and disrespects the man. His name is El Coyote. Don't you know that?"

"Fuck him. How did he kill her?"

"I wasn't there. I don't like violence. I'm a man of peace. And in any case, I can't see. I know he took her out in the woods, and there I guess he stuck her with a knife and cut off her head. That's his style. It's his thing, man."

"It's his thing?"

He grinned. "Yeah, man. He told me, in Mexico, when they see a body with the head missin', they say, 'El Coyote has been this way.'"

NINETEEN

I MET DEHAN IN THE CORRIDOR AND WE MOVED DOWN to the coffee machine. We stood looking out the window at Main Street and the gabled roofs that poked out from among the pines on the slope above it. There were a few wafts of woodsmoke trailing out of the chimneys. It was kind of idyllic, and for a moment I understood Watson, and why he didn't want to believe that his people could be like Sly, and Coy, and Greg.

I asked her, "How's Cowboy Carson?"

She shrugged. "He's scared, but he says he hasn't got anything to tell us. How about you?"

"Sly says Coy did it. His story more or less matches what we thought. Only trouble is, he's not much of a witness, being blind. In any case, he says he wasn't there at the killing, and the rest of it is mostly hearsay."

"Great."

"Yeah, listen, you take Sly now. Get him to go over his story a couple of times, see if there are any inconsistencies. Have a deputy draft it, then have him sign the statement. If I'm not finished with Greg by then, have Sly taken down and get Coy up here."

"Got it."

She went into interrogation room two, and I went to check

my laptop for the records. There was still nothing. I went in to Greg. He looked scared. I sat opposite him and said, "I suppose Detective Dehan has made you aware of the situation."

"Yeah, she's made me aware of the situation. But I am going to say to you what I said to her. You are making a big mistake."

"How's that?"

He leaned forward. "I don't know what Sly and Coy got up to in New York and Mexico, but that don't have nothin' to do with me. I ain't no goddamn killer!"

"That's not the way it looked last night. I was there, remember? You told me you whipped somebody to death."

He sighed. "You have to understand, Detective. I meant to put a scare into you. That's the way we do things 'round here. Somebody treads on your toes, you gotta put a scare into them, or they'll walk all over you. I threw a scare into you and I hurt you, and maybe that was wrong. But I never meant to kill nobody!"

"You bullwhipped me, and now you are asking me to be understanding and sympathetic?"

He swallowed and flopped back in his chair, staring at me. I was looking across the table at the man who had caused me more physical pain than I had ever believed possible, and I wondered whether I could remain objective. He was close to panic.

"Look," he said, "I have a reputation 'round here. I have to look tough . . ."

"You don't look so tough right now, Greg."

"No, I know, I understand that, and I understand that I made a big, *big* mistake last night." He leaned forward again. "Not just last night. I made a big mistake getting involved with those boys. I should never have done that. But, see, I didn't think no harm would come from selling a bit of weed. You know, if it's legal here, it can't be that bad, right? And I'm told everybody smokes it in New York anyhow."

"The law of joint enterprise holds that all three of you are equally guilty."

He took a deep breath and held the edge of the table, trying to control himself. "I know that, and I am admitting to you that what I done was wrong . . ."

I cut across him, "Who killed Kathleen Olvera?"

He stared at me. "*I don't know.*"

"Right now, while we are talking, Sly is next door giving a statement to my partner."

He went pale. "What's that son of a bitch sayin'?"

I smiled. "I'll bring you a transcript, shall I? He wants to make a deal with the DA." I sighed and sat forward, with my elbows on the table. "You have to realize, Greg, that all three of you are going down. You're all facing the death penalty. Detective Dehan must have explained that to you. Now, that is the reality you have to face. We have irrefutable proof of what you did. Now one thing, and one thing only, is going to earn one of you leniency, and that is the name of Kathleen's killer."

His face flushed and there were tears in his eyes. He leaned forward. "If I knew, do you think I wouldn't tell you? I liked Kathleen! Her an' Pat was like sisters to me. I was real fond of 'em both. If I didn't help you, that's only 'cause I don't like strangers butting their nose into our business. But I cared for both of 'em. And when Pat got in trouble with Sly and Coy, I bailed her out. You ask 'em."

I made a face like he was boring me. "Come on, Greg! You must have some idea. You picked her up from the bus station and delivered her to the Shack!"

He screwed up his face. "What? *When?*"

"The weekend she was killed."

"That's horseshit! I never picked her up. How could I? I didn't even know she was comin'."

I pinched the bridge of my nose and tried to ignore the headache that was developing in my temple.

"Pat owed Sly and Coy money."

"Yes, sir. She did. Five grand, according to Sly."

"You paid?"

"On one goddamned condition. I told them plain. If they

hurt a hair on her head, I would bullwhip . . ." He faltered. I gestured him to continue. "That's what I said to them. If they hurt Pat, I would bullwhip them to within an inch of their lives. I paid them the money and told them not to use her no more for distribution." He shrugged. "That was when we started talkin' about doing a more businesslike operation."

"But Coy wasn't happy with that arrangement. He wanted to make an example of somebody."

"Coy is full o' shit. He talks big, like he was a hit man for some big Mexican gang. But he's just a junkie loser like Sly. I told him stay away from Pat, and that was the end of it."

I shook my head. "Your story doesn't make any sense, Greg. If Coy wasn't threatening Pat, then why the hell did Kathleen come to the Shack?"

"I don't know. It's what I keep tellin' you. I didn't even know she was comin'."

"Would she have told you?"

"'Course she would've! Especially if it was to stop Coy hurting Pat!"

I stared at him a long while. "I have a witness who is willing to testify that you drove down to Boulder on Sunday, the eighth of July, to pick Kathleen up from the bus station and deliver her to the Shack." He was shaking his head. I raised my voice, leaning forward. "You yourself corrected me when I said she'd arrived by train. You *told* me she would have had to go to the bus station! You picked her up and you delivered her *to her executioner!*"

"*No!*" He made to stand but couldn't because of the cuffs. He shouted again, "*No! Goddamn it! I wouldn't do that to Kath!*" He sat staring at me, breathing heavily. "*It never happened!*"

There was a knock on the door and Dehan poked her head in. "Sly's gone down." She glanced at Greg. "He made his statement. Coy is on his way up."

I studied his face. "Think it over."

He shook his head. "I ain't sayin' another word without my lawyer."

I nodded to Dehan. "Have a deputy call Mr. Carson's lawyer, will you?"

"He's on his way already."

I stood. "See you at trial, Greg."

I stepped into the corridor. El Coyote was led past to interrogation room two and then they took Greg down to his cell. I stood staring at Dehan, chewing my lip. Eventually I said, "There is something wrong."

She frowned. "Sly was pretty convincing. You don't believe him? He confirmed your theory."

"Let's talk to Coy."

We went in, and Dehan leaned against the wall while I sat. He watched me with his pale blue eyes. The scar gave him a twisted look of contempt, but it was there in his eyes too. It was almost a palpable thing.

"I'm going to make this easy for you, Coyote. All three of you are facing the death penalty. You understand that?" He nodded. "Your pal Sly is trying to cut a deal with the DA. Greg is waiting for his lawyer, and you and I both know what his lawyer is going to advise him to do."

"What deal?"

"I need the name of the man who killed Kathleen."

"So you gonna seek the death penalty for two of us, but the one who gives you Kathleen's killer, he gets life?"

"That's the deal."

He nodded. "That's what I figured. It was Greg."

"What?"

"Greg killed Kathleen."

Dehan spoke from behind me. "Bullshit."

He stared at her with no expression. "What, you want me to say it was Sly? It weren't Sly. Sly don't go killin' people. That ain't his scene."

"How about you?"

He looked at me like I was crazy. "Me? What the fuck do I wanna kill that bitch for? She ain't nothin' to me."

Dehan came and sat next to me, leaning across the table. "She disrespected you. She didn't pay what she owed you."

"You confused, Detective. That was her sister, not her. Pat didn't pay. But Greg paid for her. All square."

"But you wanted her punished."

"You crazy. We got the farm on Greg's land. We growin' the crop on Greg's land. He's supplyin' the seeds. Greg says, 'Leave Pat alone,' we leave Pat alone. I ain't gonna jeopardize a sweet thing like that to punish a stupid bitch. She's Greg's bitch, that's cool with me. So long as he pays."

I stared at him a long time. Finally, I asked him, "So, what happened?"

He shrugged. "Is like you said. He went down to collect her from the bus station. He brought her to the Shack. He was mad at her. I don't know why. I think he liked her and she went and married another guy. I don't know. I wasn't interested . . ."

I interrupted him. "But, if she wasn't there pleading for Pat, why the hell was she there?"

"Don't ask me, man, ask Greg. All I know is, Sunday he went to get her from Boulder. Then he brought her to the club. He raped her right there on the floor. Then he stabbed her with his knife, cut off her head, and took her out to the woods."

"And you witnessed this?"

"Yeah, man. I saw the whole thing."

"You understand that if you are lying, perjury will be added to the charges against you."

He spread his hands. "What you fockin' want, man? You ask me to tell you who killed Kathleen. I'm tellin' you and now you say I'm lyin'! What the fock is the matter with you?"

I made him go over the story another couple of times in more detail, then got a deputy to come in, take it down, and have him sign it. Then I sent him back down to his cell. I grabbed some coffee and me and Dehan went to the small office where I'd put my laptop. This time there were two emails. One contained the phone, email, and credit card records. The other was from Frank at the lab. I had them printed, and ten minutes later, we sat at the table and went through them.

The phone records for the end of June and early July showed no communication between Kathleen and anybody in Colorado. She had not telephoned, or been telephoned by, her in-laws, Greg, or anybody else. Her WhatsApp showed the same thing, as did her Facebook account. She had not been conducting a "virtual" affair with Greg.

Her credit card records showed no train ticket purchases for the months of June or July—or plane or bus tickets, or car rentals.

I sat in silence, thinking, for a long time. Then I looked at the results of the DNA test and closed my eyes.

"My God, Dehan," I said, "I have been so blind. I have been so *stupid!*"

I threw the paper across the desk to her. She examined it, frowned, and stared at me.

"What the hell . . . !"

I nodded. "Let's wrap up here and get back to New York."

TWENTY

THE ASSISTANT DISTRICT ATTORNEY ARRIVED SHORTLY after lunch, and she and the sheriff joined us upstairs in the small office. She was in her midthirties and living the dream in an Italian suit and a German car. When she strode in, Dehan had her ass on the windowsill and I had my feet on the desk. We were staring at each other in silence, thinking, and both turned to look at her and the sheriff as they entered.

She dropped her pigskin case on the desk and sat. The sheriff said, "This is Assistant District Attorney Susanne O'Connor." To her, he said, "Detectives Stone and Dehan of the NYPD, ma'am."

I took my feet off the desk and rolled a little closer. She spoke first. I got the impression she always spoke first, and last.

"I'm a little confused, Detective Stone, on a number of points. First of all, why you are here at all, and, not least, I have just arrived to hear that the case you were about to close is not closed at all. Care to explain yourself?"

I studied her face for just long enough to make her uncomfortable. Then I said, "You're confused?" I turned and smiled at Dehan, who smiled back. "The assistant DA is confused, Dehan. She doesn't know why we are here." I turned back to the ADA.

"I'd suggest the sheriff explain, seeing as it was him who invited us to come here, but frankly, I think he's as confused as you are."

Her cheeks had gone a pretty shade of pink. "I'm not sure I like your tone, Detective."

"That's okay, you don't need to. Why we are here is irrelevant to the case you are going to prosecute, which is not the murder of Kathleen Olvera. That case is going to be prosecuted in New York. The case you are going to prosecute is the kidnapping, torture, and attempted murder of two police officers who were here at the invitation of the Lee County sheriff, as well as the illegal sale of cannabis in New York State. If you are curious as to why we are here, then I suggest you get Sheriff Watson to explain it to you over coffee and blueberry pie. You ready to play nice now, or you want to keep measuring dicks?"

O'Connor went scarlet, and I heard Dehan snort and splutter behind me. The sheriff hitched his pants and said, "Hey now . . . !"

She rose to her feet. "I will not tolerate . . . !"

"Sweetheart, I got bullwhipped last night and was within half a second of having my throat cut while doing this clown's job, so you will tolerate whatever you have to tolerate. You be civil to me and I'll be civil to you, but tell me to explain myself one more time and things could get ugly. Now sit down and I will tell you what happened."

She sat back down with wide eyes and a small bump.

"Five years ago, a decapitated woman was found on Lefthand Canyon Drive, not far from a club called the Shack, frequented by off-gridders and Hells Angels. The woman was eventually identified as Kathleen Olvera, from the Bronx. Her family had been regular visitors to Seven Hills since she was a kid, they had befriended local people, including Greg Carson and the Olvera boys. Eventually she married Moses Olvera, and he and his brother moved to the Bronx. You with me so far?"

She gave a tight-lipped nod. The sheriff pulled over a chair and sat. I went on.

"Sheriff Watson made a preliminary, cursory investigation. He turned up no meaningful evidence and the case went cold. A few days ago, he kicked it back to us and we started to look into it. At first it looked to us as though Kathleen had come to Seven Hills to meet with somebody, and that somebody had killed her. So, at the express invitation of the sheriff, we began to look into the people whom she might have come to see. Are you still following me?"

"Yes, Detective. It is not that complicated."

"Good." I said it a little sourly. "I wouldn't want you to get confused."

"You have made your point."

"In the course of our investigation, we turned up two things: first, Greg Carson and two of the tenants on his ranch, Sly and El Coyote, otherwise known as . . ."

I turned to Dehan, who checked the printout we'd got earlier from their NI numbers. "Juan Fernandez and Sylvester Thelonius Jones, both originally from the Bronx, in New York."

"These three characters had set up business, growing very substantial amounts of cannabis on Greg's ranch, and selling it illegally in New York. Their idea was that Pat, who was something of a black sheep in her family and had a taste for the wild side, would market it back east. The problem was that Pat started snorting all their profits instead of handing them over to Greg, Sly, and El Coyote. The penalty for that kind of thing where Sly and El Coyote come from is very severe. That led us to the theory that Pat might have sent Kathleen to intercede on her behalf and ask for clemency. And they decided to make an example of her."

O'Connor nodded and glanced at the sheriff. "That was what I had understood from Sheriff Watson."

"Yeah. We seemed to have it in the bag. And this morning, faced with the threat of the death penalty, we had Sly pointing the finger at Coyote, and Coyote pointing the finger at Greg. The trouble is, they lied. They told me what they thought I wanted to hear in the hope of getting a deal. Neither of them was able to describe the murder correctly. Plus . . ." I spread my hands. "You were right, Sheriff. You were right for the wrong reasons, but you were right. She was not killed here. Her body was dumped here, and I think she was decapitated here. But she was killed somewhere else. Greg, Sly, and Coyote are guilty of trafficking marijuana, of kidnapping, and attempted murder, but they are not guilty of the murder of Kathleen Olvera. Somebody else did that."

We showed her the video evidence and signed sworn statements as to what had happened the night before, and by four o'clock we headed back toward Seven Hills to pack our bags and start home for New York. On the way, as we wound through the forested canyons, Dehan said, "The decapitation . . ." She turned in her seat to frown at me. "Are you sure about this? It was Coyote's trademark. It was on his doorstep. He had motive . . ."

"Motive?"

"To send a message to Pat. You said so yourself."

I nodded. "I know. But I was wrong. It happens." I grinned at her. "Not often, so don't get used to it. But I was blinded by the obvious, by the details, and I didn't see the bigger picture."

"Show me the bigger picture."

"For a start, suppose Coyote was so mad he decided to make an example of Kathleen. That is a totally believable scenario and it *could* have happened. But why not then go after Pat? He knows the Bronx. He grew up there. He has Angels he can call on who can find her and make the hit, or break her arms or whatever. Why kill her sister but leave her? What message does he send by doing that?" She made a face and nodded. I answered my own question, "Not so much, 'Wherever you hide we will find you and punish you,' as, 'If you take the trouble to come to the remotest corner of the United States, right to our front door, we will kill you.'"

She smiled. "I see your point."

"As to the decapitation, it is not exactly Coyote's trademark." I raised an eyebrow. "Assuming his boasts are true, he kills his victims by stabbing and decapitating them with a knife, all in one savage attack. That's what makes him so scary. But Kathleen was beaten and strangled—not stabbed. And she was decapitated *after* she was killed, probably with a machete. Remember, it was a single, clean cut. By the way the head had rolled away from the body, I'm willing to bet that cut was delivered after the body was dumped." I paused and looked at her. "Which is suggestive."

It was, as the sheriff was fond of saying, ten miles as the crow flies, but twenty-five with all the twists and turns through the canyons. We took the short route, via Lefthand Canyon Drive, and after a long silence, as we turned left out of Gold Hill, headed finally for the Wagon Wheel, Dehan said, "Suggestive. Suggestive that whoever dumped the body knew about El Coyote's signature and wanted to cast suspicion on him."

"It's possible."

She puffed out her cheeks and blew. "So, if that's right, and that is a big 'if,' it narrows our pool . . ."

I shrugged. "It was pretty narrow already, by the simple fact of where she was dumped. I'd say that it confirms the pool rather than narrows it."

"Okay. So we are looking at somebody who knows about Lefthand Canyon, who knows about the Shack and Coyote's reputation, and about Kathleen's association with this place. All of that points . . ."

"To her family."

"So the question becomes, out of that small group, who benefited from her death?"

"That's what we are going to look into as soon as we get back, but a couple of people leap out at you, don't they?"

"Three names jump out at me, Stone. In terms of who benefits, Mo and Anne-Marie had reason to want Kathleen out of the way. And Mo's friendship with Greg and Pat means he was very likely to know about Coyote's signature."

She hesitated while I pulled up and parked outside the hotel. I killed the engine and looked at her. "And the third?"

"Pat. Pat was the one with the most intimate knowledge of this place, the Shack, Sly, and Coy. But I can't think of a motive for her."

"I agree. But there is a lot we don't know yet. Intimate relationships are the ones that breed the strongest and darkest motives for murder. And in my experience, relationships don't come much closer than sisters."

We climbed out, and I stood looking around me at that mini, bucolic utopia nestled among the mountains. I muttered, "This other Eden, demi-paradise, this fortress built by Nature for herself against infection and the hand of war."

"What's that?"

"Shakespeare. He was talking about England, but it kind of describes this place, doesn't it? A fortress built by Nature against infection. But you are never more at risk than when you feel safe. Betrayal, the betrayal of those who are close to us, those whom we love and believe love us. That is the greatest danger of all."

She put her hand on my shoulder. "You want one more bison steak and a night of rest and healing in demi-paradise before we head back to the infected lands, or you want to go home now?"

I thought about it. "Five a.m. gets us to the Forty-Third at eight a.m. the next morning."

"Makes sense to me."

I called the captain as I climbed the steps.

TWENTY-ONE

THE DRIVE BACK WAS TEDIOUS AND UNEVENTFUL. WE ended up stopping, around midnight, at a motel near Lake Erie and sleeping for four hours. Which meant we finally pulled into the 43rd Station House at noon. The first thing we did was drop in on the captain for a debriefing. He was less than amused by the fact that we had, arguably, entered Greg Carson's property illegally, but satisfied that we had "assisted" the county sheriff in busting a drug trafficking ring.

"But," he said, gazing out the window at the fall leaves on the plane trees. "If I understand you, John, the sheriff of Lee County asked for your assistance because he did not believe the murder was committed there. You went there believing it was, and effectively proved that he was right in the first place. So you are now back at square one. Would you say that is a fair assessment?"

He narrowed his eyes at me, but it was Dehan who answered.

"It's not a fair assessment, Captain."

He shifted his gaze to her. "It's not, Carmen?"

"No, sir. In the first place, Sheriff Watson had done squat. He kicked it back to us because he said he hadn't the resources to investigate, but in fact he had simply assumed that the murder took place here. He didn't prove it, he assumed it. Our investigation not only busted a drug ring that was selling dope in New York, we also found evidence, related to that ring, that will assist in clearing up the case. Evidence the sheriff should have uncovered himself."

"I see. So what is your next move?"

I took a deep breath and sighed. "I want to know what life insurance Kathleen had and who benefited from it. So we'll be talking to her insurance company. I also want to talk again to Mo and Anne-Marie. They are the obvious beneficiaries of her death. Presumably *he* benefited from any life insurance, and they both benefited because they were free to marry."

He frowned. "I thought you'd looked at that and discarded it."

I nodded. "Yes, and it still doesn't make a lot of sense. Why kill her but divorce Isaac? But still, we have to look again because we obviously missed something."

"Okay, perhaps her life insurance, assuming she has any, will provide an answer."

Back downstairs, while Dehan went through Kathleen's file to find out what policies she had, I called Mo and told him I wanted him and Anne-Marie to come over to the station for a chat. He said they'd be there by one.

When I hung up and looked across the desk at Dehan, she had a face like brain-ache. She tossed a sheet of paper on the desk in front of me. It told me Kathleen did indeed have a life insurance policy, it told me how much for, and who the beneficiary was. I stared at it for a long moment, then tossed it back.

"Find out who took it out. Mo and Anne-Marie will be here in half an hour. I'm going to talk to Mo. I want you to take Anne-Marie. Don't lean on her. Be nice. Be understanding, woman of the world stuff. Ask her what she knows about Kathleen's movements the morning she was supposed to have left. Go over it in detail, step by step."

"Okay. Are we telling them we know she didn't go to Colorado?"

I shook my head. "No. Let them think we still believe she was killed out there. All we are trying to do is piece together her movements that morning. I want them both relaxed and off their guard. Then I want to compare their stories. So press her for details, as many details as you can. That's where the devil is, in the detail. And that's where they might start contradicting each other."

They arrived at five past one. We greeted them cordially and said we'd be more comfortable upstairs where no one would disturb us. Mo looked a bit disconcerted when Dehan led Anne-Marie away, but I smiled and assured him we just wanted to discuss different things, and this would save time.

I led him into the interrogation room and we sat. He leaned on the table and asked me, "How'd it go in Seven Hills?"

"Inconclusive so far. I wanted to ask you about Kathleen's movements on the Friday morning that she left for Colorado. But before we get to that, tell me something. What do you know about a guy called El Coyote . . . ?"

He smiled. "Coy? He's a friend of Greg's. I don't know much. I believe he's some kind of wetback, if you'll forgive the expression, Detective. He likes to make people believe he ran with a Mexican gang when he was younger, likes to play the hard man. I don't know if it's true. Folks up in the mountains ain't easily impressed, if you take my meaning."

I smiled. "Yeah, I noticed. So you don't know if his stories are true?"

He gave his head a little twitch. "I don't know. He liked to play with knives, and he used to tell this story that he was known in Mexico for cutting folks' heads off, but I never gave it much credit, to be honest."

"Yeah, that's what I'd heard." I nodded. "Okay, Mo, what I really want to talk about today is Kathleen's movements before she left. First of all, how did she travel, and where to?"

"Well, to be honest, Detective, I have never been sure. See, we'd had a bit of a fallin' out, on account of she thought I wasn't spendin' enough time with her and Baby. So she didn't actually tell me *how* she was goin'. She just said she was gonna go see my parents. I always assumed she took the train or the bus. But she might have flown, I suppose. Or she might have rented a car."

"Okay. So talk me through what happened that morning."

"Jeez." He gave his head another twitch. "It's a long time ago, but I'll do my best." He thought for a moment. "I recall I had spent the night at Mom's place."

"Why was that?"

He looked a little surprised. "Well, I had to be up early to go with Isaac. He had a friend who was maybe gonna give me some work. So I had to be up early and Baby, bless her, she was keepin' us up all night."

I nodded understanding. "Sure, I get it. But you didn't go with Isaac in the end."

"Oh, well, uh, no. He phoned to say he'd got up late. So we'd go on Monday."

"Okay, so what time did you get home?"

"Well, I can't remember exactly . . ."

"Did you have breakfast at home?"

"Uh, yeah. I reckon I did, yeah."

"And how was Kathleen over breakfast?"

"Like I say, she was a bit mad at me for havin' left her alone."

"Did you often get mad at each other at that time?"

"No!" He laughed. "Most of the time we was inseparable. Everybody used to comment on it, how close we was. We never had what you'd call a fight. We was real close."

"So what happened after breakfast?"

He shrugged. "We talked a bit. She told me she was mad and she told me why . . ."

I interrupted him. "Now, I'm a little confused. You said she was mad because you hadn't been spending enough time with her and Baby—Sinead, right?"

"Yeah."

"But you just said that you were real close . . . So how come you hadn't been spending time with her?"

"Well, no, I mean, it was just that night. Maybe a couple of other nights, if I had to be up early."

"Okay, so she told you why she was mad, and what happened then? How come you didn't make up?"

"Well, she said she was goin' up to see my folks."

"Did she often do that?"

"No."

"Had she ever done that before?"

"Not really."

"Not really . . . ?"

"I mean, never."

"Did that strike you as strange, Mo? Her suddenly up and going off to see your folks like that?"

"Well, I guess it did. But she was mad, and women can do real strange things when they're mad."

I laughed. "You got that right! And it sounds like she was pretty mad!"

He laughed with me, relieved at the drop in tension. "She was that!"

I stopped laughing and frowned. "Odd though, isn't it, that she was *that* mad. You know, you say you had a great relationship, never had fights, and yet she got so mad about you staying at her mom's place . . . Doesn't seem much to get that mad about."

He swallowed. "I guess . . ."

"So she was real mad, and not in the mood to make up and kiss."

"Nope."

"So what happened next?"

"Well, uh . . . She left. Said she was goin' to see my folks and have a break for a few days. And she walked out."

I nodded and thought about it for a while. Then I stood and said, "Will you excuse me for five minutes, Mo? I'll be right back."

He looked a little anxious. "Sure . . ."

I stepped into the corridor and walked down to the room where Dehan was talking to Anne-Marie. I poked my head in and they both looked up. I smiled at Anne-Marie, then said to Dehan, "A word?"

She came out and closed the door behind her.

"Give me five minutes with Anne-Marie, will you? Take Mo. Just make him go over again, in minute detail, what happened on the Friday morning, and where he spent Thursday night."

She frowned at me. "Care to tell me what we're doing?"

I nodded. "As soon as I know, I'll tell you. Just go with it for now."

She walked down the way I'd come, and I stepped into the room with Anne-Marie, closed the door, and sat opposite her.

"Anne-Marie, I want to make this as painless and simple as possible. Nobody is judging anybody here, we are all adults. All we are doing is trying to unravel this mess and get at what happened to Kathleen up in Lee County . . ."

She frowned at me. "What do you mean?"

I smiled and placed both hands on the table. "Okay, Mo has just come clean with me and told me that you and he were having an affair before Kathleen's death." I laughed. "I have to tell you that that came as a surprise to absolutely nobody!" She laughed nervously. I went on in a reassuring voice. "Now, I know that he spent the Thursday night with you, he told me. So what I need you to do is confirm that for me, and tell me exactly what happened on Friday morning."

She hesitated, then flopped back in her chair, smiling. "Oh, Lord! That's kind of a relief. It's like a weight off my chest to be able to admit that." I smiled and waited. "Yes, Mo spent the night with me. And then next morning he went back to his apartment . . ."

"I don't mean to be indelicate"—I gave her my best lopsided, man-of-the-world smile—"but being in the first flush of a new romance, that would have been what, about eleven in the morning?"

She blushed and gave a pretty, demure laugh. "About that, yes."

"Now, just clear something up for me, Anne-Marie, how did this work? Isaac . . . ?"

I paused so she would fill in the gap. She obliged. "Isaac stayed in our apartment and me and Mo stayed at Mel's."

"And Mel?"

She sighed. "Things had got real bad between me and Isaac, and I had been stayin' at Mel's most all the time for about a month, I guess. She's real fond of me and I am of her too. So I had my room there and everything. Well." She grinned and winked. "Mo slept . . ."—she made speech marks with her fingers—"'on the couch,' and he'd sneak up to my room when Mel was a'bed."

I nodded. It made perfect sense.

I stood. "Thank you, Anne-Marie. You have been very helpful. That's all I needed to know for today. If you want to wait downstairs, your husband will be out in a moment."

She went down, and I went back to where Mo, looking slightly ruffled and irritable, was talking to a very stolid and impassive-looking Dehan.

I sat next to her and stared Mo in the eye. "You should have told me that you were sleeping with Anne-Marie before you split up with Kathleen." He made like a goldfish for a couple of seconds and I carried on. "Lucky for you, Kathleen was killed in Lee County. A lie like that puts you right up the suspects list." He swallowed hard. "Pat still lives with your mother, right?"

He nodded. "We all do."

"That's cozy."

"We're a close family."

"She work? She go out?"

"Not much."

"Okay, you can go. Your wife is waiting downstairs."

He got up without saying anything and hurried out. I sat for a while staring at the empty space Mo had recently occupied. After a bit, I turned and looked at Dehan. I said, "I'll be damned."

She nodded. "You probably will be. Feel like cluing me in yet?"

I shook my head. "Let's go and talk to Pat. It's high time we did that."

TWENTY-TWO

In the car, headed north and east toward Morris Park, Dehan turned in her seat, with her back against the door, and watched me drive. Eventually, she said, "I guess it's no great surprise, right? It's usually the husband. Or the wife. And that's what you're thinking, right? Mo did it. That's why he lied about his affair with Anne-Marie."

"Put all the pieces together."

"Yeah, if I could just find the straight edges and the corners I'd do that."

"Mo pretended he was *not* with his wife on Thursday night. How many husbands have you come across who pretend they were *not* with their wife when they *should* have been with her?"

"You have a point, not many."

"Where was he?"

"With Anne-Marie."

"So she is his alibi."

"Oh. I see. So it's both of them. That's pretty standard too."

"But we arrive right back at the same question. Why divorce Isaac, but kill Kathleen?"

She groaned and flopped her head back. Then narrowed her eyes at me. "You know, don't you?"

I eyed her sidelong and imitated an English accent. "I have taught you my methods, Watson. Observe and deduce. Eliminate the impossible . . ."

"I know, and whatever is left, however improbable, is the truth."

I pulled into Van Nest and parked outside Mel's house. We climbed out of the Jag and I stood a moment, smelling the first hint of frost on the air as the sun slipped behind the treetops, where copper leaves were beginning to wither and fall. We pushed through the gate into her garden, climbed the stairs to her door, and rang the bell.

Mel beamed at us. "Well, look who it is! Isn't it Detectives Stone and Dehan! Well isn't that a lovely treat all the same. Will yiz not come in and have a cup of tea? I was *just* putting the water on! Baby's just having a nap upstairs."

She bustled in toward the kitchen as Dehan followed her and I closed the door. We heard the tap and the water splashing into the kettle.

"Can't you feel the cold in the air? It'll soon be Christmas and it's not Halloween yet. Doesn't time just fly!"

I stemmed the flow. "Mrs. Vuolo. We're actually here to talk to Pat. Is she in?"

"*Pat?* Yes. Isn't she in her room? She's just after going up. Go on. I'll call yiz when your tea's ready. Go on! It's the last door on your left."

As we climbed the broad stairs she called after us, "Will yiz have some biscuits? I have some nice chocolate biscuits. Will you have some?"

We told her we would and arrived at the landing. It was an ample, galleried affair with five bedrooms and a bathroom leading off it. We went to the last one on the left. I could hear the sound of a muffled TV inside. I knocked.

"What?"

"Pat, this is Detectives Stone and Dehan, from the New York Police Department. Can you spare us five minutes of your time?"

For a moment, nothing happened. Then the door opened and she peered out at us. She was short and very thin. Her skin was pallid and her eyes were hollow, as though from too much sleep and not enough sun. She had a woolen hat on her head, a stud in her nose, and fingerless gloves on her hands. Her nails were bitten. "Cops?" I nodded, and we showed her our badges. "What do you want?"

"Can we come in? It's easier than talking on the landing, or shouting through the door."

She stared at me a moment. "I guess." She stood back to let us in. "The room's a mess."

It was, and it smelled of stale sweat, tobacco, and weed. The sheets were rumpled, and her two chairs were covered in unwashed clothes. She sat curled up on the bed and switched off her TV. "Just throw the clothes on the floor. I have to wash them anyhow."

We did as she suggested and sat. I studied her a moment. She was probably thirty-two or -three, though her skin looked older; but her manner was that of a teenager. She said, "What do you want?"

"We're from the cold-case unit at the Forty-Third Precinct, and we are investigating your sister's murder."

"No shit."

"I was wondering if there was anything you could tell us about that?"

She shrugged. "No?"

"The night before last, Sly, Coy, and Greg were arrested in Lee County, for drug trafficking and attempted murder . . ."

Her jaw dropped, and her face, which had been ghostly, turned a whiter shade of pale. "Who . . . ?"

"Me. They tried to kill me, and Detective Dehan." I waited a moment, and she seemed to try and crawl inside herself. "We are not Vice, Pat. We are not interested in the part you played in selling the dope here. We are only interested in your sister's murder. Do you understand that?"

She nodded.

"Good. I just have a couple of questions for you. I want you to think back five years, to just before Kathleen's death. Things were pretty tough back then, financially, right?"

"I guess."

"Your dad was dead . . ."

She nodded.

"Mo had lost his job."

Again she nodded.

"So it was just Kathleen and Isaac earning. Is that right?"

"Uh-huh . . ."

"And you."

She swallowed.

"You were making money selling Sly and Coyote's merchandise."

She nodded. "We needed it pretty bad. That's the only reason I did it."

I smiled sympathetically. "You were pretty young, and from what I've heard, pretty wild back then. Is that true?"

She smiled uncertainly. "Back then. Now I just smoke a bit of weed. Mom don't know about it. You won't tell her, will you?"

I shook my head. "So, business was beginning to go well. You were making a few grand on each shipment. No questions asked at home, everybody grateful, and Greg, Sly, and Coy happy as Larry." She nodded, looking sheepish. "But then you blew it. Or should I say snorted it. What was it, a night? A weekend?"

"A long weekend."

"How much did you blow?"

"Five grand." She giggled. "It was wild. I just wish I could remember it."

"Were you scared of what Coy might do to you?"

"Yeah, pretty scared. I didn't think he'd kill me or nothing, but he'd beat me up before, for having the wrong money, or not doing things right. Greg told him to lay off and he did. But I knew he was gonna be real mad about this. I was pretty sure Greg would too."

"What about your mom and Mo and Anne-Marie?"

She was quiet for a bit, just looking at me. Eventually she said, "They were mad too. Especially Anne-Marie."

I stood and walked to the window. The drapes were drawn, but I moved them with my finger and looked out. In the gathering dusk I could see the large, well-tended garden. The lawn was freckled with October leaves, and a wind, which I could imagine touched with ice, was rattling a few that still clung to the silver branches of the trees. The shed stood at the end of the garden. Sheds are to Brits and the Irish what garages and basements are to us. They are places where guys go to escape from wives and mothers. It's where they go to smoke, drink beer, and play with power tools.

"Who uses the shed, Pat?"

"We have a gardener, he comes once a week. But mainly it's Mo. It's his shed and his tools."

"That's what I thought."

We left her in her room. As Dehan closed the door we heard the TV come on again, and Mel's voice came up the stairs. "Are yiz done already? I was just bringing up the tea. Will you have it in the parlor?"

I smiled warmly at her. "That sounds wonderful, Mel. Now, while you and Carmen have a chat, do you mind if I have a peek in your toolshed?"

She shrieked with laughter. "Whatever for?"

"Like your son-in-law, I am a DIY nut. I cannot see a toolshed without going in and having a snoop. You don't object, do you?"

She looked confused for a moment, then shrugged. "The key is there, by the window. The switch is inside the door."

I crossed the lawn and unlocked the wooden door. I pushed it open and felt for the switch. The light was from a single bulb with a green shade that hung suspended from the ceiling. It was neat.

He had a workbench on the right, with all his tools hung on a board. There was a smell of creosote and sawdust. At the back, there was a lawn mower and a collection of digging tools, a hose on a reel, and a pitchfork. On the left, there were a couple of chairs and a wood burner. There was also a small fridge. Two got you twenty there was beer in there. Under the bench, there were three plastic storage crates, and I knew that's where it would be.

It was buried under everything else at the bottom of the box, but it didn't take long to find it. It was in a black canvas bag with a drawstring. Using my handkerchief, I extracted the machete from the bag and took a photograph of it. The blade was still stained. I put it back in the sack and replaced it where I had found it. Then I sent the photograph to the captain, with a message. *Was given permission to look in shed at Melanie Vuolo's house. Found this. Please get warrant to search property and seize evidence for tomorrow AM.*

I switched off the light and locked the door, then went back inside. Mel and Dehan were in the parlor drinking tea. Dehan's face bore a rigid rictus, while Mel, oblivious, talked about every and any thought that, like a butterfly on a late summer breeze, wafted into her mercurial consciousness.

She jumped up and smiled, clasping her hands, joshing and poking fun at me as I came in. "Well, was it everything you hoped it would be?"

"That, and much more."

She turned to Dehan. "Men! Simple minds are easily pleased!" She squealed and slapped my arm. "*Simple minds are easily pleased!*"

Dehan stood, and she clung to her arm. "*Simple minds!*"

Dehan laughed, put her arm around her, and shook her head. "I know, easily pleased."

"We must go," I said.

"And you never had your tea."

"It's an excuse for me to come back."

"Ooh, you're a charming divil, so y'are!"

"You won't say that when I come back."

She laughed again and we left, stepping into the cold evening air. The door closed behind us, and we made our way to the car, with our breath fleeing before us like urgent ghosts. And it wasn't even Halloween yet.

TWENTY-THREE

OCTOBER HAD FINALLY DECIDED TO START MOVING toward winter. It was nine thirty in the morning, and there was frost on the road and on the lawns, giving the green grass in the front gardens a silvery glint. Dehan and I climbed out of my Jag as the uniforms climbed out of the two patrol cars: Karen and Bret, Sean and Lou. Even the echoes of the slamming doors sounded icy. There was some foot stamping and hand rubbing, and with hunched shoulders we climbed the steps and rang at the door.

Dehan had with her a shoulder bag.

Mel opened the door with her usual big smile, but as she caught sight of the four cops behind me and the paper in my hand, her smile faded into incomprehension. "Detectives, for the love of God, what is it?"

I handed her the warrant. "Mel, I have a warrant to search your house and the shed in your back garden, and to seize any evidence pertinent to my case."

She looked stunned, then stepped aside. "Surely you could have just asked . . ."

The uniforms filed in. Dehan sent Karen and Bret upstairs and told Sean and Lou to wait. I paused a moment with Mel. "I'm sorry, Mel. It has to be this way. I called Mo last night and asked him not to go to work. Are they here . . . ?"

"I'm here, so's Anne-Marie. What is this all about?"

He was in the kitchen doorway, staring at me. I turned to Dehan. "Can you gather everybody in the parlor, Detective Dehan? I'll join you in a moment." I turned back to Mel. "This won't take long. I just need to ask you all some questions. Where's Sinead?"

"She's at the nursery, God love her . . ."

Pat appeared on the stairs, accompanied by the two cops. She looked even more pale and scared than she had the evening before.

"Mom? What's going on?"

Mel's face was bitter. She looked me over from head to foot, like she was seeing the real me for the first time. "It's all right, love. It's some kind of misunderstanding. They'll be gone soon."

Anne-Marie appeared at Mo's elbow, and everybody was shepherded into the parlor. I turned to Sean and Lou. "Go in there with them. Nobody leaves."

"You got it, Detective."

They stepped inside and closed the door.

"Karen, Bret, get Pat's cell phone and her laptop and take them over to the lab. Tell Frank to go through her social media, her emails, her calls and text messages, everything. We are looking for communication between her, Greg, Sly, and Coyote. Then come back."

"Got it."

"Okay, Detective Dehan, you are with me."

I took the key from where I had left it the previous evening and we crossed the garden to the shed, with the morning frost crunching under our feet. We let ourselves in and pulled on our surgical gloves. Dehan took a large plastic evidence bag from her pocket.

The machete was where I had left it, in its canvas sack at the bottom of the crate. I laid it on the workbench, withdrew the blade, and laid it on top. In the morning light, it was clear that the steel blade still had gore on it. Dehan reached in her shoulder bag and pulled out a camera and a bottle of luminol. She set up the camera on a small tripod on the bench, and I closed the door and the shutters on the window, then dowsed the light. She sprayed the blade, and as it started to glow blue, she took a long-exposure photograph.

"It's blood," she said.

"Next thing is to prove it's hers, and that his prints are on the handle."

"Why the hell would he keep it? Why didn't he ditch it?"

I shook my head. "You'd need a psychologist to answer that one, but I'm guessing it's some kind of trophy. The moment he decapitated his wife, it obviously meant something to him. Some kind of liberation, or triumph."

She bagged it and the canvas sack separately and we took them inside.

Everybody looked up as we stepped into the parlor. Mo and Anne-Marie were sitting on the sofa together, holding hands. Pat was curled up in one armchair and Mel was in the other. She looked mad, but the other three looked scared.

They had a fire burning in the grate, and opposite it, between the sofa and the two chairs, was a coffee table. I laid the machete on it and looked at Mo. His eyes were like saucers and he was very pale. I glanced at Anne-Marie, then at Mel and Pat. They were all staring at it with no expression at all. Then they all looked at Mo.

"That's blood on the blade, Mo. That's a nice Micarta handle, composite of linen and paper. It's expensive, but it looks good, and it's comfortable, right?" He was staring at me. He didn't answer, so I went on. "It will also hold a fingerprint for years. In about half an hour, Officers Bransen and Murphy will return, and they will take this machete, and the canvas sack, to the lab for analysis. I am willing to bet they are going to find the blood is Kathleen's and the prints are yours. Have you anything to say, Mo?"

The entire room seemed to have gone into some kind of catatonic shock. I looked at Mel. She was transfixed, staring at her son-in-law. Anne-Marie was still looking at the blade.

Finally he gave a big blink, like he was dragging his mind back from some nightmare. He said, "No. *No!* This is wrong. You are lying to me." He pointed at the weapon. "That is *not* her blood. And you cannot prove it is. It is not possible."

Anne-Marie gave her head a quick shake. "He's right. You're trying to trap him. There is no way you can prove that is Kathleen's blood."

Dehan folded her arms. "Why not?"

Mo went to answer, but Anne-Marie cut across him fast. "Because in the first place, it ain't hers! And in the second place, even if it was, after five years it would be so deteriorated it would be useless."

She smiled. "You an expert in forensics, Anne-Marie?"

Anne-Marie scowled at her bitterly. "We all are. When you are the victim of this kind of crime, you become an expert in all sorts of things you never expected. Look at the semen they found in Kathleen! The poor girl was raped, and after just a few days the sample had become unusable. You want us to believe that after five years, the blood on that blade will give you a DNA profile?"

I raised an eyebrow. "Is that how old it is, five years?"

She went pale and stammered, "If it were, it would be . . ."

I walked to the bow window and rested my ass on the windowsill. I crossed my arms and stared at Mo for a moment. "I'm glad you brought up the subject of the semen, Anne-Marie. It's something that has been troubling me. You see, when I talked to you both yesterday, you lied about where Mo had spent the night."

She came back quick. "We didn't lie, we just didn't tell the whole truth. He did spend the night at Mel's house. We just didn't mention we were having an affair at the time, until you tricked us."

I scratched my chin. "But here's the thing, Mo. If you spent the night with Anne-Marie at Mel's place, and the next morning

—you say first thing, Anne-Marie says around eleven—you went home, argued with Kathleen, and she left, at what point exactly did you have sex with her?"

His face had gone the color and the texture of a church candle. "I don't know what you're talking about."

"Yes, you do, Mo. DNA technology is advancing faster than you can imagine. We resubmitted the semen sample for testing and they got a match. It was yours. You had sex with Kathleen just before she died."

Mel closed her eyes. "Jesus, Mary, and sweet Joanna!"

Anne-Marie had turned and was staring in horror at her husband. "You did *what*? What kind of . . . ?" She stopped herself and turned to me. "Is this true or is it another trick?"

Dehan said, "Think about it, where did he spend the night?"

She turned furious eyes on her husband. Her hands were trembling. He was shaking his head.

"I swear, baby. It ain't true. I promise you."

Mel's voice came like she was biting each syllable as it came out.

"Don't—say—another—*word*!" She glared at me as though I had somehow betrayed her. "Lies! Lies and trickery! He is a good lad! Him *and* Isaac, God love 'em both! They stood by me when Kath was taken from me, and I will *not* believe these *lies*! Lies and feckin' trickery! *Ashamed* of yourself, you should be!" She turned back to Mo. "Not another word, you hear me?"

I watched her a moment before answering. Her cheeks were flushed and her eyes were bright. Her mouth was a hard line and her jaw was stubborn. "He raped and murdered your daughter, Mel."

"*Mrs.* Vuolo, to you! I will not believe it. I will not! How you could do this to us after what we have already been through. *Shame! Shame* on you!"

I looked back at Mo. Anne-Marie had removed her hand from his and had crossed her arms. She had tears in her eyes.

"How about it, Mo? You ready to tell the truth? What are we

going to find when we analyze the machete? You know, and I know, that your only hope now is leniency in sentence. And the only way you are going to get that is by coming clean. Tell me what happened, Mo."

Mel's face had started to crumble. Her cheeks were wet. She was staring at Mo, appealing to him. "You didn't do it, Mo. Tell me you didn't. I'll believe you. We'll get you a good lawyer. Don't say nothin' till we get a lawyer. We'll get through this, love, like we got through everything else. Stick together. Remember? That's what we promised each other. A family. Stick together . . ." Her lip curled, and she buried her face in her hands and started to sob, begging God to help them.

I sighed. "Here's what happened, Mo. Anne-Marie had already broken up with your brother. You were the one she had always liked, anyhow. And you were getting a bit tired of Kath. She'd served her purpose, which was to get you to the big city. But now she was becoming a pain in your ass. I don't know exactly why, maybe she was a Goody Two-shoes. Maybe she was a bit too puritanical. Maybe it was just that she now had a baby . . ."

Pat's voice was startling in its suddenness and the venom it contained. "Maybe it was all those things . . ."

Mel turned on her. "Pat! Don't you *dare*!"

I raised my eyebrows at Mo. "Maybe it was all those things. Point is, you were ready to move on. One of the things that had me and Detective Dehan scratching our heads was why you didn't just divorce her. But we'll come back to that a little later. For now, let's just say that you couldn't."

Mel turned her large, wet eyes on me, and her twisted, wet mouth. "He couldn't because he loved her. Please, I'm begging you, stop attacking my family . . ."

I ignored her and went on. "I'm guessing you'd spent a few nights with Anne-Marie at Mel's place already. She'd been staying there since she had split up with Isaac. And even though you were unemployed, and Kath was the one who had to get up for work, you used the excuse that little Sinead would not let you sleep so you could go there and spend the night with your mistress.

"But that night was different. That night you stayed home. What did you do? Pretend you were hoping for a reconciliation? Or were you just on some kind of power trip?" I pointed at the machete. "The fact that you kept that, as a trophy, with her blood on it, that tells me it was probably a power trip. I think you bludgeoned her, raped her while she was half-conscious, strangled her, and then took her downstairs to your car. I think you dumped her in the trunk and you drove her all the way to Lefthand Canyon."

He said, "That's ridiculous . . ." but his voice faltered as he said it.

"One of the things that confused me right from the start was, if she was going to Seven Hills, how the hell did she wind up ten miles away, back of beyond in that canyon? We assumed somebody must have picked her up from the bus station and taken her there. But then we found she had never even gone there, never bought a ticket, never caught the train.

"But you, you knew all about Lefthand Canyon, you knew all about its reputation as a place where people dumped bodies, and they could go for years without ever being found." I paused and shook my head. "And if you hadn't been so arrogant and lazy, you might have got away with it. But instead of burying her, you were on some kind of power trip, weren't you? You knew about El Coyote's reputation and you thought you'd be smart. So when you dumped her, you cut off her head and left her half-buried to be found and cast suspicion on Coy. It was a stupid move."

Mel had collapsed, convulsing and sobbing, repeating over and over that she did not believe it. She refused to believe it. Mo was staring into my face. I held his eye for a long moment. I knew he was ready. I said, "That is what happened, isn't it, Mo?"

He nodded. "Yes. But I ain't gonna say another word till I have a lawyer."

TWENTY-FOUR

MEL AND ANNE-MARIE WERE STARING AT MO IN horror. They were like odd mirrors of each other, their mouths sagging open, their eyes round and wide, and an odd kind of dumb stupidity about their expressions.

Mel said, "Mo, no . . ."

And Anne-Marie echoed, "How could you . . . ?"

I looked over at Dehan. She was frowning, like she was wondering if I was going to read him his rights, or if I wanted her to do it. I gave her an imperceptible shake of my head.

"I haven't arrested you yet, Mo. We'll get you a lawyer in due course." I smiled. "No doubt you can get a pretty smart one of your own." I thought for a moment. "You know, there were a lot of things that gave me a headache about this case. But one of the biggest was the way some of the things you did were smart, and threw me off—like taking her all the way to Colorado, while you and Anne-Marie provided alibis for each other . . ."

She looked at me in alarm. "I had nothing to do with this!"

I ignored her and plowed on. "But other things threw me off because they were so stupid I didn't believe anybody would do them, like raping her, or cutting off her head to implicate Coyote without bothering to find out what his real MO was." I paused, shaking my head and narrowing my eyes at him. "You could be so smart in some things, and so stupid in others. It was almost like you had a split personality. One of you was smart, and the other was just a stupid redneck. Why, for example, did Anne-Marie separate from Isaac and eventually divorce him, but you had to go to the extreme of killing your wife?"

I stared at him awhile, then shifted my eyes to Anne-Marie. She'd gone from looking outraged to looking scared again. Then I turned and studied Pat. She still looked terrified, only maybe a little more so. They didn't like the question.

"As I said, it was like two people. And when I realized that, everything began to slip into place. Talking to you, it was clear to me that there was no hidden, brilliant side to your personality, Mo. Forgive me, but you are just plain stupid. And once I accepted that, it was clear that the smart things you had done were somebody else's idea.

"So, I didn't have to look very far, did I, Anne-Marie? Now, my next question was, what makes an attractive, moderately intelligent woman like you marry a man like Mo? Even allowing for the fact that you might find him attractive, that is not enough to marry him, is it? So, what would be enough to make you marry him?"

She swallowed. "I love him . . ."

I snorted. "You married Isaac for the same reason that Mo married Kathleen, to get out of Seven Hills and start a new life in the city. And, like Mo, once you were here, your partner became a millstone 'round your neck. It was easy enough to walk out on him, but hell, you needed somewhere to go. Well, that wasn't too hard. You and Mel had become close. So you could go to her, right?"

There was absolute silence. I spread my hands. "But that got me thinking. It didn't make a lot of sense. Her son-in-law is walking out on her daughter, and she is providing a home away from home for his mistress! Providing a place for them to meet and hook up! It didn't square."

Mel stammered, "I had no idea, so help me God . . ."

I went on, "So what, how do we explain all of this odd behavior?" I looked at Pat, at Anne-Marie, at Mo. I pointed at him. "You had thrown in your job, Kathleen and Isaac were making the bare minimum. Money was in very short supply." I sighed, shook my head, and turned to look at Mel. "Especially since your insurance payoff from your first husband had started to run out. In fact, the biggest provider in the family was Pat, with her income from selling dope for Sly and Coy.

"But then she went and blew it. The one big earner you had went down the chute. And Greg made it clear. He would protect Pat from El Coyote, but he was cutting her off. She would not sell for them anymore. Your goose had laid her last golden egg. What to do?"

Mel had gone very still. I pointed at her. "You know? You are one of the most charming people I have ever met, Mel. A bit too charming. Because one of the first things that struck me when I first met you was that, even though I was there to discuss your daughter's murder, rape, and decapitation, all you could think about was whether I would have a cup of tea and a biscuit." I gave a small, humorless laugh. "It wasn't like she'd died twenty years ago." I frowned. "Even then, it wouldn't have made much sense. But five years? After such a brutal murder? And then I started to put the pieces together: you provided a home for your son-in-law and his mistress; you moved, from a small house on Rosedale Avenue to this big, comfortable home in Morris Park, and brought your son-in-law and his mistress with you. You felt no grief, no resentment, no compunction . . . In fact, you felt nothing."

Her face was drawn, hard. "That's not true."

"When your husband died, leaving you comfortably off thanks to his life insurance, he had no idea that in doing so, he had planted the seed for his daughter's murder. The solution was simple. Mo, acting as always on your instructions, took out the insurance. To cover himself, he took it out in your name. You, the matriarch, would take care of everybody. But . . ." I laughed. "You were audacious! Two million bucks! Enough, with the sale of your old house, to move to this place and have a comfortable income for the four of you for the rest of your lives. Not luxury, but comfort. Enough to invest in a small business for Mo and Anne-Marie. Enough never to have to worry again about paying bills."

She shook her head. "No . . ."

Anne-Marie had collapsed on the sofa and had covered her face. Mo seemed to have slipped back into a catatonic state. I went on.

"But it had to be planned very carefully. "Mo and Anne-Marie would provide alibis for each other. The fact that they were both having an illicit affair would explain away any secretiveness on their part, any reluctance to be forthcoming or give details about their movements.

"Dumping the body in Lee County was clever. I'm pretty sure that was down to you, Mel, right? Not only was it a different jurisdiction from where the crime had taken place, it was a remote jurisdiction with few resources. So a major investigation was never likely to get under way. It was just another unexplained body dumped in Lefthand Canyon. If Sheriff Watson hadn't kicked it back to us, if Mo hadn't beheaded her, if he hadn't kept the machete, we might never have got this far.

"And even the insurance was smart. Mo never figured as the beneficiary. And the beneficiary was not only her mother, but did not even take out the insurance, and could claim ignorance of it." I sighed. "But the monthly premiums, they were what gave it away. Kathleen was on such a limited income. Mo had *no* income. And the premiums on a two-million-buck insurance policy are high. So the three of you were splitting the payments. It's right there in your bank records. The three of you set up the insurance, knowing that you were going to kill her. That takes a very special kind of evil, Mel. A very special kind of coldness."

She turned to look at me and her eyes were hard and cruel. I believe if she could have killed me right there and then, she would have.

"It was for the best. Her and that streak of parrot's piss, Isaac, were never going to get us out of that shithole we was living in. Sure, wasn't Kath living in one feckin' room with a bathroom, and wasn't Isaac and Anne-Marie the same? What way is that to live? She was better off dead. The only ones with any balls to try and get out of the mess was Mo and Anne-Marie!"

"And me . . ." I turned. It was Pat, staring at her mother with a pleading face. "I did my best . . ."

Her mother looked at her with venom in her eyes. "Ah, feck off, you gobshite! If it wasn't for the likes of you, we'd not be in this mess in the first place! And you!" She scowled at Mo. "If you'd done it like I said, we'd've got away with it, you stupid, feckin' eejit!"

I stood. It was as good as a confession. "Melanie Vuolo, I am arresting you for conspiring in the murder of your daughter, Kathleen Vuolo. You do not have to say anything, but anything you do say may be taken down and will be used in evidence against you in a court of law . . ."

"Feck off!"

As I put the cuffs on her, I could hear Dehan reading Mo and Anne-Marie their rights too. Through the window, I could see Sean and Karen pulling up to collect the machete. They climbed out of the patrol car, breathing billows of condensation as they talked and laughed, moving up the garden path. It was a cold day.

EPILOGUE

"YOU OUGHT TO BUY A DISHWASHER. EVERYBODY HAS dishwashers these days."

She was standing at the sink with the cold light of a winter afternoon on her face, slowly washing a plate. She seemed abstracted. On my laptop, Dean Martin was singing that the weather outside was frightful, but he reckoned the fire was quite delightful. I had to agree. I hadn't lit it for over two years, but now it looked festive and homely. My house hadn't looked homely for a long time.

"It helps me to think," I said as I poured two martinis and contemplated the tree. It looked like a badly wrapped Christmas present. I liked it.

"Washing up helps you to think?"

"Uh-huh."

She was quiet for a bit. The smell of baking moussaka began to creep out of the kitchen. "I know she was a crazy bitch, and what she did to her daughter was unforgivable, but I hated testifying against her." She sighed. "She's plausible. If it hadn't been for the strength of the evidence against her, I don't think the jury would have convicted her."

"I agree." She was drying her hands and I handed her her drink. "Cheers!"

"Cheers!"

We drank.

She went through and stood looking at the fire and the tree for a long while. "Family," she said at last. "They have such power to hurt you, because you need them so much."

"I guess so."

She turned to face me. I was struck, not for the first or the last time, by how beautiful she was. But I paused this time, to observe that the beauty came as much from the honesty and intensity of her gaze as from the perfection of her features. Then I buried the thought.

She said, "Do you miss your family?"

I shrugged. "I have no family left. But I guess I do miss having a family. If I think about it."

She smiled. It was a sad smile. "I miss having a family. I miss my mom and dad. They were nice."

She sat on the sofa, opposite the fire. I sat in the chair and watched her. "Two weeks to Christmas, Stone. What will you do?"

"Read a book. Watch a movie. I don't know. How about you?"

She shrugged, pulled a face, and shook her head. "Same."

"You not going to your uncle's?"

"You kidding? No way!"

We sat in silence for a little longer, not sure whether to ignore the elephant that had just strolled into the room. In the end I shrugged one shoulder.

"You want to come over? We could read a book and watch a movie together."

She smiled at the tree, then grinned without looking at me. "Yeah, why not? Depends on the movie . . ."

"*Wizard of Oz*."

"I love that movie."

"And then *Terminator Two*."

"Oh, man! Yeah! But no rom-coms!"

"Agreed."

"How about board games? You like board games?"

"Christmas pudding and backgammon."

"You don't wanna play backgammon with me, Stone. I will *destroy* you!"

"Oh, really? Ha! Think again, Ritoo Glasshopper, you nevah praid a mastah before . . ."

The fire crackled and spat lazily as the aroma of moussaka gradually permeated the house. We talked and laughed, and challenged each other amiably in the warm glow of the flames and the sparkle of the overdressed tree. And after a while, I poured the wine as she pulled the moussaka from the oven and set it on the table with the carrots and the broccoli. We drank too much and laughed at things that only we could find funny, and the sun set and the darkness enclosed my small, warm house. And as the fire died to embers, we went up to bed: me to mine, and her to the guest room, which was hers.

Don't miss THE HEART TO KILL. The riveting sequel in the Dead Cold Mystery series.

Scan the QR code below to purchase THE HEART TO KILL.

Or go to: righthouse.com/the-heart-to-kill

NOTE: flip to the very end to read an exclusive sneak peak...

DON'T MISS ANYTHING!

If you want to stay up to date on all new releases in this series, with this author, or with any of our new deals, you can do so by joining our newsletters below.

In addition, you will immediately gain access to our entire *Right House VIP Library*, which includes many riveting Mystery and Thriller novels for your enjoyment!

righthouse.com/email

(Easy to unsubscribe. No spam. Ever.)

ALSO BY BLAKE BANNER

Up to date books can be found at:
www.righthouse.com/blake-banner

ROGUE THRILLERS
Gates of Hell (Book 1)
Hell's Fury (Book 2)

ALEX MASON THRILLERS
Odin (Book 1)
Ice Cold Spy (Book 2)
Mason's Law (Book 3)
Assets and Liabilities (Book 4)
Russian Roulette (Book 5)
Executive Order (Book 6)
Dead Man Talking (Book 7)
All The King's Men (Book 8)
Flashpoint (Book 9)
Brotherhood of the Goat (Book 10)
Dead Hot (Book 11)
Blood on Megiddo (Book 12)
Son of Hell (Book 13)

HARRY BAUER THRILLER SERIES
Dead of Night (Book 1)
Dying Breath (Book 2)
The Einstaat Brief (Book 3)
Quantum Kill (Book 4)
Immortal Hate (Book 5)
The Silent Blade (Book 6)
LA: Wild Justice (Book 7)

Breath of Hell (Book 8)
Invisible Evil (Book 9)
The Shadow of Ukupacha (Book 10)
Sweet Razor Cut (Book 11)
Blood of the Innocent (Book 12)
Blood on Balthazar (Book 13)
Simple Kill (Book 14)
Riding The Devil (Book 15)
The Unavenged (Book 16)
The Devil's Vengeance (Book 17)
Bloody Retribution (Book 18)
Rogue Kill (Book 19)
Blood for Blood (Book 20)

DEAD COLD MYSTERY SERIES
An Ace and a Pair (Book 1)
Two Bare Arms (Book 2)
Garden of the Damned (Book 3)
Let Us Prey (Book 4)
The Sins of the Father (Book 5)
Strange and Sinister Path (Book 6)
The Heart to Kill (Book 7)
Unnatural Murder (Book 8)
Fire from Heaven (Book 9)
To Kill Upon A Kiss (Book 10)
Murder Most Scottish (Book 11)
The Butcher of Whitechapel (Book 12)
Little Dead Riding Hood (Book 13)
Trick or Treat (Book 14)
Blood Into Wine (Book 15)
Jack In The Box (Book 16)
The Fall Moon (Book 17)
Blood In Babylon (Book 18)
Death In Dexter (Book 19)
Mustang Sally (Book 20)

A Christmas Killing (Book 21)
Mommy's Little Killer (Book 22)
Bleed Out (Book 23)
Dead and Buried (Book 24)
In Hot Blood (Book 25)
Fallen Angels (Book 26)
Knife Edge (Book 27)
Along Came A Spider (Book 28)
Cold Blood (Book 29)
Curtain Call (Book 30)

THE OMEGA SERIES
Dawn of the Hunter (Book 1)
Double Edged Blade (Book 2)
The Storm (Book 3)
The Hand of War (Book 4)
A Harvest of Blood (Book 5)
To Rule in Hell (Book 6)
Kill: One (Book 7)
Powder Burn (Book 8)
Kill: Two (Book 9)
Unleashed (Book 10)
The Omicron Kill (Book 11)
9mm Justice (Book 12)
Kill: Four (Book 13)
Death In Freedom (Book 14)
Endgame (Book 15)

ABOUT US

Right House is an independent publisher created by authors for readers. We specialize in Action, Thriller, Mystery, and Crime novels.

If you enjoyed this novel, then there is a good chance you will like what else we have to offer! Please stay up to date by using any of the links below.

Join our mailing lists to stay up to date -->
righthouse.com/email
Visit our website --> righthouse.com
Contact us --> contact@righthouse.com

facebook.com/righthousebooks
x.com/righthousebooks
instagram.com/righthousebooks

EXCLUSIVE SNEAK PEAK OF...

THE HEART TO KILL

CHAPTER 1

IT WASN'T RAINING. IT WAS A DELUGE. THE RAINDROPS exploded on the blacktop on Simpson Street, raising a mist of spray two feet from the ground. The early-morning crowds were bent and hunched under their umbrellas, not so much hurrying as fleeing from the downpour. I watched Dehan through the windshield as the wipers squeaked and thudded in their losing battle against the water. She stepped out of her apartment block, warped wetly as the wipers swept past, then regrouped and walked around the hood of my car. Instead of an umbrella, she had on an Australian leather hat and a long coat. She pulled open the door and climbed in with a self-conscious grin on her face.

"G'day, Bruce!"

I smiled, shook my head, and pulled away. "Bruce?"

She removed her hat. Her hair was tied in a knot behind her head and now she tightened it as she spoke. "Didn't you know that, Stone? Australians call all men Bruce, and all women Sheila. It's a thing. So I say, 'G'day, Bruce!' and you say . . ."

"G'day, Sheila. Never let me say you didn't teach me anything." We drove in silence for a moment, among the hiss, the squeak, and the thud, the wet noises of a January morning in

New York, and the warm sigh of the heater. "I was looking at the David Thorndike case last night," I said. "I'd like to review it."

She frowned. "Thorndike. Wasn't he the journalist?"

"Investigative journalist on the *New York Telegraph*. Found murdered in the apartment he shared with his girlfriend on Manor Avenue, at eleven a.m. on the eighth of March, 2008 . . ."

"Last seen?"

"The night of the sixth, Thursday, by his girlfriend, at about nine p.m."

"So no precise time of death?"

"Nope. Sometime between nine p.m. Thursday and eleven a.m. Saturday. Thirty-eight hours. No forced entry. Only access to the apartment was through the front door. He had been shot, once, in the head at short range . . ." I turned and smiled at her. "With his own 9mm Glock."

"He was shot with his own Glock? That's not cool."

"It's not polite at all, is it?"

"No. How about forensics?"

"Squat. The prints in the apartment were his, his girlfriend's, the landlord's, and a couple of others that got no hits on IAFIS. The only prints on the weapon were Thorndike's."

"Obviously, they ruled out suicide."

I nodded. "He was lying in the middle of the floor, on his back. Entry wound was center of his forehead. The weapon was left on the bookcase by the door. The slug, found on the carpet a few feet away, matched the weapon."

She snorted. "I guess that's pretty conclusive. So the killer was admitted voluntarily, got access to Thorndike's Glock, then shot him with it. One single, clean shot."

"It certainly looks that way, yeah."

"What about the girlfriend?"

"Katie O'Connor, she was out at a restaurant with a guy, paid with her credit card, tight alibi."

"Anything taken?"

"Yes, no, maybe. There were no signs of robbery as such.

Their money, his wallet, credit cards . . ." I made an "and so on" gesture with my hand. "All of that was untouched. In fact, it looked like the whole apartment was untouched. It was as though he simply arrived, shot him, and left . . ."

"Except he used Thorndike's own gun, so he was presumably there long enough to get a hold of it."

"That, and also his laptop and all his research were missing."

She sat frowning at her Australian hat, turning it around in her hands, like it wasn't the hat she'd expected to see there. "That doesn't make a lot of sense." She raised her frown from her hat to the windshield as I turned from 169th onto Franklin, among the ugly redbrick monoliths, made even more unlovely by the low gray skies and the broken lights on the wet blacktop.

"I guess we're not going to the station," she said.

"I thought we'd go and see his wife."

She gave one slow nod. "Okay, so this is not straightforward."

"No."

"Let me sum up what I understand so far." She hesitated a moment and glanced at me. "Are we headed for Manhattan?"

"Yup. 104th and Columbus. It is the apartment he shared with her, which she now shares with her new husband."

"Am I playing catch-up here? Do you already have an idea . . . ?"

I shook my head. "Ideas, I have a few, but then again . . ." I shrugged. "Too few to mention."

"Funny. So Dave is married, he's doing okay because he has a nice address on the Upper West Side. For some reason you will no doubt disclose in your own good time, he also had an apartment in the less desirable Manor Avenue, in the Bronx, which he shared with his girlfriend. He's an investigative reporter, you mentioned his research and his laptop were missing, so I'm going to go out on a limb and say he was investigating a story 'undercover' or whatever the journalistic equivalent of undercover is."

"That's my girl."

"Either as part of his cover, or because he's a real dawg, he shacks up with Katie O'Connor. Then one day, somebody turns up and rings at the door. It seems he knew the caller because it looks like he let him in. The caller got possession of Dave's Glock, apparently without a struggle, which adds to the impression that Dave knew his caller. The caller then very coolly popped a cap right between Dave's eyes, without leaving prints on the gun." She shrugged and pulled a face. "It was early March, he was wearing gloves." She shrugged again, only half satisfied with her own explanation. "He then puts the gun down on the bookcase, collects the laptop, and all Dave's papers, and leaves with them."

"That's about the size of it. We have to assume also that his killer knew that Katie would be out and Dave would be alone."

We crossed the Third Avenue Bridge in silence and followed it onto East 129th, toward Harlem. Then she started nodding and spread her hands. "Okay, so I'm going to state the obvious. It looks like he was killed for the article he was writing, or because of the article he was writing, or both."

I laughed. "You're covering all your bases, huh, Dehan?"

"Yuh. But things are not always what they seem. That's what you're always telling me, right? And it may also be that he was killed by his wife, or his girlfriend, or both, and the disappearance of his laptop and his papers is incidental to the murder itself."

"Agreed."

"Does she know we're coming?"

"Yeah. I called her last night. She's an editor on a fashion magazine. She said she'd be working from home today."

We followed Central Park North onto Cathedral Parkway and then turned left onto Columbus. I parked outside the deli, she shoved her hat on her head, and we made a run for the entrance to the block. In the elevator, as I shook the water from my hair, she grinned at me from under her absurd hat.

"Who's laughing now, huh, Sensei?"

She opened the door almost immediately and looked at us with angry eyes. She was tall, as tall as Dehan or maybe taller. It was hard to tell because of the huge mop of Afro hair on her head.

Her skin was dark, but her features were more Indian than African, her eyes were almond, and her nose was long and aquiline. The expression on her face was pure Latin American, but when she spoke, her accent was English. I guess it has become a small world, and almost all of it was present there in that woman.

"Yes?"

We showed her our badges and I made the introductions. She sighed and seemed to sag.

"Look, is this going to take long? I am really busy."

I raised an eyebrow at her. "I don't know how long it's going to take, Mrs. Thorndike . . ."

"Petersen. I married again. And it's Ms."

"Ms. Petersen. We only have a few questions, but we would appreciate it if we could come in."

She sighed again, with a little less irritation than the first time, and stepped aside. "I'm sorry. Come in."

The apartment wasn't big. There was an open-plan living room and dining room, with a kitchen separated by a pine bar. Most of the far wall was taken up by a large plate glass window that overlooked the gardens on West 104th. The furniture looked like IKEA. A door beside the kitchen led to a short passage where I guessed there was a toilet and a bedroom. She gestured us to a sofa and sat on the edge of an armchair. She didn't make herself comfortable.

"I honestly doubt there is anything I can add to what I told the detectives when it happened." She shrugged. "It's almost ten years ago. Since then I have remarried and started a whole new life. This really is *not* very welcome."

I nodded and made a face like sympathy. "But you understand, Ms. Petersen, we can't just let people get away with murder because our investigations are unwelcome to the victims' ex-spouses."

She looked embarrassed. "Of course." She sighed for the third time and spread her hands. "What would you like to know?"

Dehan came straight out with it. "Where were you when David was killed?"

She took a deep breath, held it, and puffed out her cheeks. She gazed at the rain-spattered window for a moment, at the heavy clouds, and then blew out and shook her head. It was elaborate, but it looked genuine. "It was ten years ago, Detective. I don't honestly know. Besides, from what I recall, they didn't know exactly when he was killed. Wasn't there a window of twenty-four hours or something?" She kind of winced. "I think I spent the evening with friends. They must have asked me at the time. Whatever I told them then holds true today."

I nodded. "Sure. When did you first realize that David was having an affair?"

Her face went hard. It may have been ten years, but the anger was still fresh.

"I was informed by the investigating detectives that he had been shacked up with some tart when they came to interview me. That was the same day they found him, in the afternoon."

Dehan was watching her carefully. "When was the last time you saw him?"

Again the long stare at the heavy, gray sky. She bit her lip and gave her head a couple of small shakes. "It's so hard to be precise. Even at the time . . ." She frowned at Dehan. It looked to me as though she was searching for some kind of female sympathy. "He'd be gone for weeks on end sometimes. I got used to it, the way you get used to an ache. At first it hurts, then it's annoying, and finally you just forget it's there."

I smiled like I understood. "Can you give us a rough idea?"

"It must have been a couple of weeks at least. We had this . . ." She made a face that was eloquent of everything along the bitterness, resentment, disappointment spectrum. "*Arrangement*, for what it was worth. He would often disappear for several weeks when he was investigating a story. He was a good journalist . . . He was a low-down piece of *shit*! But he was also a good journalist, very dedicated and very thorough. But we agreed that we would meet at least one day at the weekend during the periods that he was away . . ."

Dehan interrupted.

"So, excuse me, Ms. Petersen, when he was away, did he not tell you where he was going?"

"No! Good heavens no! He didn't even tell me what he was investigating. He was extremely secretive about his work. I didn't even get to see his articles until they were published."

I said, "Please go on."

She took a moment, like she was examining her memories and finding them wanting. "The first couple of weeks he'd come home on the Sunday and we'd do something. Then he would start calling instead, with some excuse. Then he wouldn't even call. In the end, I stopped keeping the weekends free because I knew he wouldn't show. I'd go out to dinner with friends, or to a show, visit my parents . . ." She shrugged.

Dehan said, "Your parents in . . . ?"

"Miami."

I smiled at her and glanced out the window. "That's one alibi I wouldn't mind checking up on right now."

She smiled back. "Yeah, I hear you."

"Ms. Petersen, is there anybody you can think of who might be able to give us a line on what he was investigating?"

"Like I said, he was very secretive about his work. The only person I can think of would be Bob, his editor on the *Telegraph*. I am guessing he had to tell him *something*, or they wouldn't have approved his expenses." Her face suddenly contracted with bitterness. "I don't know what he told his whore."

I studied the anger on her face. Ten years on and there was still rage and bitterness there. I wondered if it was enough to drive her to kill. I sucked my teeth and glanced at Dehan. She shook her head and I stood.

"Ms. Petersen, thank you for your time. We'll try not to disturb you again. If you think of anything . . ." I handed her my card. "Please give us a call. Have a good day."

Outside, the rain had eased to a drizzle, but the water cascading from the awnings and the gutters was loud and sounded cold and wet. Dehan raised an eyebrow at me and offered me her hat. "You want? It would suit you. You'd look like Indiana Jones."

"My brain cavity is larger than yours."

She snorted as I stepped out and ran for my car. She followed me at an easy walk. As she climbed into the car and slammed the door, she eyed me. "You sure about that, Sensei?"

I stared at her for a long moment. She stared back. Finally, I said, "I think she has enough rage and anger in her to drive her to kill, if the right provocation were there . . ."

"She finds out about Katie somehow, finds out where he's shacked up, goes to confront him . . ."

"It's feasible. But if she killed him out of rage, why was she so cool about it? Why the single shot? Why didn't she empty the magazine into him? Why did she remove the laptop and the papers?"

I watched her eyes move over my face as she pursed her lips. She gave a little shrug with one shoulder. "In some people, rage expresses itself as something cold and clinical. As to the laptop and the papers, like we said before, that might be something completely unrelated."

I grunted. "What d'you want to do now?"

"You know what? I'd like to see the apartment where he was killed. You think if we ask nicely, the new tenants would let us have a look around?"

I fired up the engine and winked at her. "I had a feeling you'd say that. I called the landlord last night. He's between lets. I said we'd be there just after ten."

She raised a laconic eyebrow. "Geez, Boss! You da best! You treat me *good*!"

"Don't you forget it, Little Grasshopper!"

CHAPTER 2

By the time we got back to the Bronx, the drizzle had turned to the occasional freezing drop, carried on an icy wind that made even the bare branches of the trees shiver. Dave's block was a five-story redbrick with an orange fire escape. The main entrance was a small courtyard that had been barricaded with a large wrought iron gate covered in steel mesh and topped off with sharp iron spikes.

The landlord, Sammy Gupta, buzzed us in and we rode the elevator to the fifth floor. I had brought with me a folder with the crime scene photos in it. The door to the apartment was open and I peered in. It gave directly onto the living room. The floor was covered in a rough, gray carpet. On the right there was a window, and in front of the window there was a small dining table with two chairs. Against the wall there was a sideboard, and directly in front of us there was a sofa that might have looked new when the Beatles still had pudding-basin hairdos. In front of it there was a wooden coffee table with very thin legs and a glass top, and a lower level where you could put magazines. Opposite the sofa, against the wall on the left, there was a dresser, and most of that was taken up with a TV.

Beside the dresser, there was an open door that gave onto a

bedroom. From in there emerged noises of movement. I knocked on the door and shouted, "Mr. Gupta? NYPD. May we come in?"

His voice preceded him, "Oh, yes!"

He was short and thin, in pleated pants, a white shirt, and a tank top. He smiled a lot, kept his arms permanently bent at the elbow and his head cocked slightly at a constant "ah well" sort of angle.

"Yes, please, come in, how do you do? Hello."

We showed him our badges. "I'm Detective Stone, this is Detective Dehan. We are reviewing the David Thorndike case . . ."

"Yes, yes, goodness yes, poor David. I remember it well. Very tragic. Please, tell me how I can help you."

Dehan answered him. "We'd just like to have a look around. Has the layout changed much since . . . ?"

As she asked it, I opened the folder and took out the pictures, but Sammy was already answering her.

"Well, it was ten years ago, and I like to keep things up to date, you know? But, no, it hasn't really changed much. Not at all. As you can see from the photos." He grinned.

Dehan took the top photo. It was the same coffee table and the same sofa, in the same position. She pointed to the carpet, between the table and the door, about ten or twelve feet away. "The body was there, lying on its back. The head just missed the table . . ." She stepped over and turned to face me.

Sammy was nodding. "Yes, that is correct. I opened the door, came in, and there he was, just where you are standing. He looked very surprised."

Dehan ignored him and carried on. "Which means he was standing about six or seven feet from his killer. The shot was pretty much point-blank if the killer had his arm outstretched . . ."

She took a couple steps toward me and I stretched out my hand as though I were going to shoot her. It would have been impossible to miss. She kept talking.

"So the killer was standing more or less where you are

standing now, by the door. He has the door open or he has it closed, we don't know. He's either just come in or he's on his way out. Again, we don't know. But that's where he's standing, by the door."

Sammy was nodding a lot. "Yes, undoubtedly that is correct. He had to be by the door to effect that shot. No doubt."

I looked at him and asked, "Did you collect the rent in cash?"

"Always. I would come in the first week of the month, and he was never late. Always on time, no problem. That is why I was worried when he did not open, and no message, nothing. It was not like him."

"I know it was a long time ago, but can you recall where he worked? Where he kept his computer and all his papers?"

"Oh, yes! Always on the table by the window." He pointed to the dining table. "Always over there. Whenever I am come to see him, always he was at the table by the window, smoking cigarettes, drinking coffee. Always there."

"But it wasn't there that day."

"No, and I am pointing that out to the police. They are saying, 'There is no robbery!' And I am saying, 'Well, look here! They have taken laptop, and also all his papers! What is that if it is not a robbery?'"

"Quite right. How about his gun, Sammy? Did you ever see him with his gun?"

He beamed. "Oh, yes! Goodness, yes! He was very chatty, friendly kind of chap. He invited me in for coffee one time, and I ask him, 'You are no afraid of being robbed? With expensive computer and important work for the newspaper?' And he says to me, 'Oh no! I am always take out special insurance!' And he shows me a pistol in the drawer. 'I always take precaution!' He was a tough cookie, all right!"

"And where did he keep it, Sammy?"

He pointed. "Over in the sideboard. He said he wanted to have it close when he was working."

Dehan frowned. "Why was that? Did he feel he was in danger?"

"He told me he was an investigative reporter, and the people he investigated were very dangerous characters. He always wanted to have his insurance. Always he said it like this, 'I always have my insurance!'"

I walked over to the table and stood by the chair. I looked over at Sammy and Dehan by the door. "Here? This where he sat?"

Sammy nodded. "Yes, just there where you are standing."

I tried to visualize it. He'd be sitting at the table, writing, reading, smoking, drinking coffee. There would be a ring at the door, or a knock. The gun is in the sideboard. He goes to the door. He is careful, cautious, he knows he is in danger and likes to keep his insurance handy, so he asks who it is . . .

I said, "Was there anything else, Sammy, that you thought was odd that the detectives at the time did not think important?"

He danced his head around a bit. "Well, there was one thing, maybe it is nothing, but I thought it was odd."

"What's that?"

"It looked to me like he was going to leave. He didn't tell me anything about leaving, but in his bedroom, the suitcase was unzipped and open on the floor."

Dehan frowned. "What about his clothes?"

"No, they were all in the drawers and in the wardrobe. It was just the suitcase, which would be normally, you know, in the wardrobe or under the bed. But that morning it was out, on the floor, and open, unzipped."

I thought about it for a moment, but it didn't say anything to me. Dehan asked him, "Do any of the neighbors from that time still live here?"

He did his little dance with his head again. "Well, you know, people in apartment blocks like this one, they are mainly transient. They come and they go. But yes. Me. I live on the first floor. I have six apartments in this block. I live in one and I let out the other five."

Dehan rested her ass against the back of the sofa and crossed her arms. "Do you remember much about what happened that day, Mr. Gupta?"

"Sammy, please. Everybody is calling me Sammy. I always think, if you can bring a smile into somebody's life, even for a moment, you have done something useful. Isn't it?" He looked from me back to Dehan. We waited. He went on, "You know, Detective Dehan, I have a very good memory, because I am very observant. I am noticing the little details. And, of course, after poor David was murdered, I was thinking about what I had noticed that day, and also the previous days. I offered these observations to the detective who was investigation, but he thought they were not useful."

Dehan said, "We think they might be, Sammy. We'd like to hear them."

"Surely, I will tell you. Let me fill you in." He grinned at us, like he'd phrased it in a particularly enlightening way. "You know that he was here for just over two months, and for most of that time he was sharing it with Miss Katie O'Connor, a very pretty and lively little filly! Oh, goodness! She was very alive!" He laughed. "And she was often receiving visits from her sister and her boyfriend."

I frowned. "Her sister?"

"Yes. But about a week before he was killed, Miss Katie moved out. David was very upset because he was *most* in love with her. She was very charming! Very pretty! Really most nice. But they had a big argument and she went with her sister and her sister's boyfriend or husband, I don't know, I am sorry. Then!" He held up his finger, grinning at each of us in turn. "Two days before he is dead . . ."

Dehan said, "Thursday the sixth of March."

He nodded at her, as though he approved of her choice of date. "Exactly correct, yes, Miss Katie O'Connor comes to visit, to collect some things, at about nine o'clock. I am hoping, you know, that she will stay the night and maybe they will make up, because he is nice man, and he is very much in love with her. They don't fight, but she doesn't stay. She goes. Friday everything is very quiet, but in the evening a woman comes to see him."

"A woman? There is no mention of this in the police report."

"No! I know! Because the detective thinks I am making a mistake. I am hearing the buzzer outside—you know, the intercom—because my apartment is right by the gate. So I am hearing and seeing most people coming and going. And I am pretty sure that I am hearing a woman on Friday night. I am hoping maybe it is Miss Katie come back to see David. So I am going to the door and looking through the peephole. But I can't see properly. She does not put on the light. But she takes the elevator to the fifth floor. Ten minutes later, not more than fifteen, the elevator comes down again and somebody leaves. Next morning I go up to see about the rent, he is not answering his door, I let myself in, and, oh my god! He is dead."

Dehan held up her hands. "So, hang on a second there, Sammy. Let me see if I've got this straight. Did you at any point get a clear look at this visitor on Friday night?"

"No."

"Not when they arrived and not when they left."

"No."

"So what makes you think it was a woman?"

"Oh, the intercom. I think I recognize David's voice, so I am saying, 'Oh, goodness, maybe Miss Katie is coming back!' And I am looking through the window. I can't see her, but I can hear her voice asking to be let in."

Dehan pressed him, "And was it clearly a woman's voice?"

"To me it was clear. To me it was a woman. But she spoke very softly. Too softly to make out what she said, or to be sure who it was."

I said, "So you can't in fact be certain that this visitor actually went to David's apartment."

He looked apologetic. "I am certain that it was a woman, and

I am certain that she did. But that is only my own personal opinion. I did not see it with my own eyes, no."

I nodded a few times and looked at Dehan. She shook her head. "I'm good."

I turned to Sammy. "You have been very helpful. Thank you. We won't keep you any longer."

He wished us all the very best and begged us please to come again if we were ever passing by in the neighborhood. We thanked him and left.

Outside, the roads were wet and the air was cold and blustery. It wasn't raining, but the clouds were dark and sagging overhead and didn't look as though they were about to move on anytime soon. We climbed into the car, and I fired up the engine and turned on the warm air. Dehan rubbed her hands together and said, "Did you happen to talk to Miss Katie O'Connor last night as well?"

I smiled and pulled my notebook from my inside pocket. I flipped it open and handed it to her. "No. She's a Realtor working southwest Bronx. I figured you could give her a call and fix up an appointment. That's her number." I gave a small shrug and grinned at her. "There is no need for her to know we are cops until we get there."

She nodded and started dialing. "Less chance of her suddenly remembering a nonexistent dentist's appointment if she thinks she's going to sell us a house rather than get interrogated about her boyfriend's murder."

"That was the way my mind was working."

She put the phone to her ear and stared out of the window. "So, what? Are we married and looking for a place together, or what?" I gave her my expressionless face but she didn't look at me. After a moment she said, "Oh, yes, good morning, am I speaking to Katie O'Connor?" She laughed like they were sharing a joke and said, "Hello, Katie! Listen, when would it be convenient for you to see us . . . What are we looking for? Well, we were hoping you could point us in the right direction!" She laughed uproariously again. "One o'clock? Oh, really? Oh, that sounds *perfect*." She looked at me and blinked several times. "Darling, Katie will see us at one o'clock on Howe Avenue. She is showing a *gorgeous* three-bedroom semidetached house. Darling, are you listening to me?"

I raised an eyebrow at her. "Yes, darling."

"Katie, that sounds perfect. We'll see you there at one. Let's see if between us we can get the old dinosaur to make up his mind!"

She hung up and eyed me, suppressing a smile. I took my notebook back and said, "That was unnecessarily elaborate."

"What can I do? I'm creative. When a girl is creative, she creates, right?"

"I need to dry out, get some hot coffee and a donut."

She smiled. "All these years married, and you still say the most romantic things, honeykins."

"Cut it out!"

She snorted but remained silent the rest of the way to Fteley Avenue.

CHAPTER 3

THE CLOUDS HAD BROKEN AND WERE HANGING, WHITE and wet, against a cold blue sky. An icy wind was whipping in gusts off the East River, flapping our clothes and dragging Dehan's hair across her face, forcing her to claw it back with her fingers so she could see where she was going. We leaned against the gusts and made our way up the drive, past the protruding garage, to the front door. It stood wedged open. I rested my hand on the doorjamb and looked in. Dehan rang the bell, then shouldered past me, muttering, "Door's open. We can go in." Then she called out, "*Katie? Katie O'Connor?*"

Katie O'Connor appeared in the kitchen doorway with a bright smile on her face. She had copper-red hair, deep blue eyes, and a cute spray of freckles. She was wearing a handsome tweed suit that made her look expensive. Her smile faded slightly when Dehan showed her her badge.

"Hi, Katie, I am Detective Carmen Dehan, and this is my partner, Detective John Stone. We'd like to ask you some questions about your relationship with David Thorndike."

It was a pretty brutal approach. Her whole demeanor seemed to collapse. She sagged, frowned, and said, "*What?*" Then, "No! I am working. I have potential clients arriving . . ."

"We won't take up much of your time, Katie, but it's easier if we do it here rather than at the station."

She picked up on the implied threat and sighed. "Fine, but please, make it quick. This is an open house. People could turn up at any time. What do you want to know?"

Dehan rubbed her hands and stamped her feet. "How about we start with why you two split up?"

A flash of irritation creased Katie's brow. "That was *ten years ago*!" She glared at Dehan a moment, then glared at me where I was still propped up against the doorjamb. "Can you come in, please, and close the door?"

I stepped in and closed the door behind me. Katie disappeared into the kitchen and we followed. We found her leaning with her ass against the sink and her arms crossed. Her face was flushed, and I couldn't make out if she was mad or scared. She was probably both.

Dehan rested against the door, and I went and sat on a pine chair at a pine breakfast table. I said, quietly, "Why'd you break up, Katie?"

She gave me that look women give you when they are seeing all men as one single, conjoined bastard. "Because he was a son of a bitch! Why are you asking me about this? It was . . ."

I interrupted her, "I know, ten years ago. We are a specialist cold case unit. David was murdered, so we aim to find out who murdered him. However much of a son of a bitch he was, murder is against the law. I hope you are going to cooperate with us."

It was like talking to an angry four-year-old. She stared at me with defiance in her blue eyes, and two red spots on her cheeks. Then she closed her baby blues and heaved a big, angry sigh.

"Okay, I understand, and yes, you are right, of course." She unfolded her arms, spread her hands for a moment, and then let them drop by her side. "We had been living together for a couple of months. He was a fun guy. He was very alive, dynamic, full of life and energy." She stopped and for a moment her eyes became abstracted. She looked out the window and into the back garden.

"You got the feeling sometimes with Dave that the world wasn't quite enough for him." She looked at me. "Do you know what I mean?"

I nodded. "Sure. He had an appetite for life."

"Oh, he sure had that. He was a good journalist. Tireless. He worked hard, very hard. A lot of women would have said too hard, but I supported him. I admire hard work and commitment in a person. I don't need some guy fawning over me twenty-four seven. I like to see a guy achieving something in life. So I supported him . . ."

Dehan narrowed her eyes. "Were you aware of what he was working on?"

Katie gave a lopsided smile. "No . . . Dave was super careful and secretive about his work. Nobody, and I mean *nobody* got to see it. Even his editor got the bare minimum of information."

I said, "Okay, so in what way were you supportive?"

She shrugged. "I made no demands on him—if I worked eight or nine hours a day, he would work sometimes twelve or fifteen, sometimes more. When he did, I would keep him supplied with coffee, food, whatever he needed until he was done." She shrugged. "We got up together, we went to bed together, and I was there at his side every step of the goddamned way. I believed in him."

I knew the answer but I asked anyway. "So what happened?"

"It's obvious, isn't it? I discovered the son of a bitch was married."

Dehan was chewing her lip. She said, "How'd you find out?"

She stared at Dehan for a long moment, then down at the floor. "He told me."

"He *told* you?"

She nodded without looking up. "It was about a week or so before . . . before they found him. I got home from work and he was kind of hyper. He wasn't making a lot of sense. He said the article was finished, it was going to be mega." She shook her head, still looking at the floor. "He was talking crazy stuff, about getting the Pulitzer, writing a best seller, making a fortune. At first I was right there with him." Now she looked up and held Dehan's eye. "I was as excited as he was. We were going to be rich, famous. It was going to be bigger than Watergate. Then, I remember it like it was yesterday, he took hold of me by the shoulders and told me to sit down. He sat next to me, on the sofa, and told me."

Dehan shook her head. "Son of a bitch."

Katie glanced at her. She looked grateful. "Yeah. He'd been married for five years, something like that. I don't remember exactly. I just remember going cold all over. The *betrayal*!" She stopped and studied Dehan's face for a moment, like she was searching for something there. "All the time we had been together I had thought I knew him, but he was a stranger. He'd been lying to me, using me. And what about his wife? If he was capable of doing that to her, what would he do to me in five years?"

Dehan nodded. "Suddenly, he was a stranger."

"Right. He told me he was going to come clean with her, tell her about us and get a divorce. Then we'd get married . . ."

She gave a sudden, startling yelp of laughter and leaned back, looking up at the ceiling, shaking her head in disbelief.

"Can you believe it? He had it all worked out. What he had done to his wife would just be swept away! What he was *going* to do to his wife didn't count. What he had done to me for the last two months, that wasn't important. None of that mattered anymore. Because he had decided we were going to get married. So now it was all okay."

I said, "So what happened?"

She glared at me. "What happened? I'll tell you what happened. I slapped his face and screamed at him. I told him we were finished, packed my things, and left."

"You packed your things . . . Did you have a zip-up suitcase . . . ?"

She shook her head. "No. I took most of my stuff, what I could fit, in a couple of holdalls. I left some books and CDs and went back a couple of days later to get them."

I scratched my chin a second, thinking. "Would that be the Friday?"

She raised her eyebrows. "Seriously? You expect me to remember the days of the week ten years ago?"

I managed to combine a sigh and a smile. "David's body was found on the Saturday morning. Your big bust-up would have been roughly the previous weekend."

She thought about it for a moment, then shook her head. "No. It wasn't the day before. Probably midweek, Wednesday or Thursday. I was there maybe ten minutes. Got my stuff and left."

We were quiet for a moment, then Dehan asked her, "He was found on the Saturday morning. Where were you the night before?"

Katie squinted at her. "It's got to be in the police report. Why are you asking me?"

"Could you please just answer the question?"

She sighed and raised her eyes. "Fine! I went out to dinner with a friend. They checked my alibi."

I looked out the window at the garden. The trees were nodding, and the sky had turned gray again. There were a few drops of rain on the glass.

"Katie, where did David usually work?"

She frowned, not understanding my question. "At home."

"No, I mean, where in the apartment?"

"Oh, we had a small dining table over by the window. He worked at the table."

I nodded. "I figure he had all his papers scattered around, taking up all the space, right?"

"I guess so, yeah. Why?"

"When you went to collect your books and your CDs on the Thursday, was his laptop on the table, with all the papers?"

Her face became serious. I could see she was searching her memory. I could tell it was a question she hadn't asked herself before. She frowned, then her frown deepened and she shook her head. "I'm not sure."

I nodded. "Yes, you are, Katie. Don't lie to me."

Her cheeks colored. "I don't think there was anything on the table. He'd finished the article. It makes sense."

"If that is right, where would he have put the article, and his laptop? Neither was found at the scene."

Her face was like a mask. It was as though she had climbed inside herself and she was now unreachable. She was still frowning, but no longer at my question. I had the feeling she was frowning now at her own thoughts. She said, "I don't know. I guess his editor . . ."

"Why would he give his laptop to his editor?"

"I don't know. You're asking me questions I can't answer."

"Well, what about friends? Did he have a close friend? Somebody other than you that he trusted?"

She thought, and when she answered her voice was almost a whisper. "No . . ."

"I think you're lying, Katie."

Her eyes flashed. "I am *not*! He didn't trust anybody! Not even me!"

"You're telling me he had no friends?"

"He had acquaintances. Some close acquaintances. But no friends. There was Bob, Bob Shaw. That was his editor. He was about as close as anybody ever got to him. And some guy he spoke about sometimes. I never met him. Guy called Lee. But I'm pretty sure the only person he would have trusted with his work, once it was finished, was his editor."

I thought for a bit, then sighed and put my hands on my knees. "Okay, Katie. I'm going to need an address and a number where we can reach you besides your work number. I'm pretty sure we'll need to talk to you again."

She reached in her purse and handed me a card. "Does that mean I'm a suspect? I have an alibi. It was checked."

I stood, took her card, and put it in my wallet. "Nobody has an alibi, Katie, because nobody knows at what time he was killed. Please, don't leave town."

As I opened the front door onto the icy, gray day, I heard Katie behind me. "Were you the couple who were due at one?"

I looked at Dehan, who turned to answer. She looked embarrassed, just shrugged, and shook her head.

I climbed into the Jag feeling vaguely depressed. Dehan climbed in beside me and we both sat staring at the bleak expanse of the sound, reflecting the cold gunmetal of the low clouds.

"Sucks," she said, and I nodded. "We need to eat and review what we have so far." I nodded again and fired up the old brute.

Scan the QR code below to purchase THE HEART TO KILL.
Or go to: righthouse.com/the-heart-to-kill